The Less-Traveled Road

Lawrence Ianni

iUniverse, Inc.
Bloomington

The Less-Traveled Road

iUniverse books may be ordered through booksellers or by contacting:

iUniverse
1663 Liberty Drive
Bloomington, IN 47403
www.iuniverse.com
1-800-Authors (1-800-288-4677)

ISBN: 978-1-4759-3872-2 (sc)
ISBN: 978-1-4759-3873-9 (e)

Printed in the United States of America

iUniverse rev. date: 8/6/2012

I shall be saying this with a sigh
Somewhere ages and ages hence:
Two roads diverged into a wood, and I –
I took the one less traveled by,
And that has made all the difference.

From "The Road Not Taken" by Robert Frost

This book is dedicated to my wife Mary Ellen, who started along a series of less-traveled roads with me 60 years ago, leading as often as following, often doing her own explorations, while remaining constant in kindness and support to me and our two daughters.

1

JOE BELL HAD ALWAYS been fortunate in his bad luck with women. The entire summer before his junior year in high school, he planned the approach he would make that fall to the cheerleader whom he had studied so longingly the previous fall from his spot on bench with the other substitute football players. He had plenty of time to admire her since an injury to the star receiver he would replace never happened. Though the cheerleader was a sophomore as was he, he had lacked the courage to talk to her, or any other girl for that matter. But this coming football season, he expected to be a starter, and his courage was bolstered to converse with the pretty, energetic, slim-bodied girl with the perpetual smile. Eventually, he imagined, their conversation would lead to their first date, which would be his first ever. Later, there would be an agreement to go steady. In fact, he had already extended his fantasy to marriage after the completion of high school. However, he learned just a week before school was about to begin that she and her family had moved out of the town. Thus his plan envisioning an early marriage rather than college was replaced with one focusing on his intellectual interests.

Looking back ten years later, as he stood on the front porch of his rented cabin in the Sierra Mountains of Northern California, he long ago had recognized that a marriage at age eighteen would have locked him into a lifetime of blue-collar employment and the inevitable insecurity that the early marriage of an uneducated man would have entailed.

Just two months into his freshman year of college, he had fallen in love a second time. The poised senior who riveted his attention was not a beauty, but she was extremely attractive in a wholesome way. Her auburn hair framed a milky freckled face that just failed at striking beauty because of a nose that was flat enough to disqualify the young woman as a classic beauty. At just an inch shorter than Joe's height of five feet and ten inches, she carried herself with a grown woman's maturity and confidence. Her conversation was spirited and merry, and Joe was totally captivated by her. She was amused by Joe and pleased with his attentions for several months until Joe's callowness and over-eagerness became too much for her. She ended their association when she returned to campus from the Christmas break. Joe suffered all the devastation that an eighteen year old boy could feel when he was rejected by the twenty-two year old woman of his dreams. His pain endured his entire freshman year since he could not avoid seeing his lost love almost daily on a college campus that was both small in acreage and enrollment.

The sting of the thwarted romance was sufficient that Joe was no more than a casual and infrequent dater during the rest of his undergraduate years. When he studied for his masters in journalism, all the women he was tempted by were as career focused as he. Neither he nor they confused their short passionate interludes with love. This mode of encounter continued to be the case for Joe during his first job as an all-purpose reporter for a small town daily. When the poor pay of newspaper work prompted him to seize the opportunity to become a copywriter for a large advertising agency in San Francisco, he met Andrea. She was an account executive for the same agency for which he wrote copy while starting to wonder if his skill with language and his love of using it might be put to more satisfying use writing fiction.

His early attempts at short stories were so wooden that he dared not expose them to other eyes. However, his ad copy won enthusiastic approval from both account executives and the agency's clients. Andrea was among those who were impressed and took the trouble to know him beyond nodding acquaintance. Joe was delighted because he had found the tall, flawlessly formed and featured woman enticing from the day he had first seen her. His casual acquaintance with Andrea deepened into serious interest when he found their mutual interests went far beyond shoptalk to a similar taste in books and music. Without discussing commitment, Joe and Andrea dated exclusively for six months.

Just as Joe began to think of marriage for the first time since his freshman year of college, Andrea told Joe in a burst of excitement that he was about to be offered a promotion into a beginning level management position at the agency. Joe was less than excited. Although writing copy was not an inspiring career, it was tolerable. The thought of managing people and projects conjured tasks that went beyond unpleasant to repellent. Andrea could not understand Joe's lack of interest. She emphasized that he was being offered the first rung on a career ladder that could lead to senior management, perhaps even leadership of an entire ad agency eventually.

Senior level management was a goal Andrea aspired to herself one day, and she could not understand why Joe did not see the potential of the opportunity that was about to be offered him. When Joe admitted to Andrea that he did not want to remain a copywriter all his life, Andrea was more intensely puzzled at his distaste for a management career. Joe could do no better than to explain that it was a fine goal for someone like herself who wanted it, but that it was an unattractive choice for him.

Andrea never told Joe that their relationship was over; she was abruptly no longer available to him until he got the message. The agency was large enough that it took little effort to avoid their crossing each other's path. In retrospect, Joe realized that Andrea's condemnation of copywriting as a tolerable career somehow lessened his tolerance for the job. He returned to short story writing as a nourishing activity. When his courage was up to making freelance submission of his work, he got full and frequent exposure to the coldness and brevity of the standard printed rejection note. In time, he received an occasional one sentence personalized rejection slip which encouraged future submission. This was enough to convince him that he ought to make a serious attempt at being a publishable writer of fiction. When he had added enough to his savings that he could afford to live frugally for a year without salary, he quit the advertising agency and literally headed for the hills of California to make writing his full time activity for as long as he could afford to.

Joe felt lucky to have found the cabin which he had occupied for the last month. Though the monthly rent was a bit more than the most modest and remote rentals in this region of the Northern California mountains, he had gotten a favorable rate by leasing for a full year. The cabin itself was a wood frame square consisting of a living area, a kitchen and two bedrooms, the smaller of which Joe used as his work room. The bath had reliable plumbing and a satisfactory shower. Joe had no neighbors closer than a half mile, though his cabin sat on the outskirts of the town of Craterville, a village of about a thousand people that was built astride state route 110. Route 110 was a two lane road that climbed from the five thousand foot level in Craterville to near the top of a ridge of peaks in the high Sierra, where it dead-ended.

One feature of the situation of Joe's cabin seemed unlike the mountain retreat that it truly was. His front porch did not look out on an expansive view of downward-sloping, forested mountain sides. In fact, Joe did have a beautiful and extensive view. However, he looked out on the continuous circle of a mountain ridge encircling the town of Craterville and submerged it at the bottom of a 1500 foot bowl. Joe's cabin sat on the beginning of the upward slope of a side of this bowl. Standing in the middle of Craterville, one had the impression that one was standing in the caldera of an immense extinct volcano. It was this feature of the locale that had prompted the first settlers to choose the name they had given the town. Although geologists had later established that there had been no volcano that had formed the terrain, none of the town's residents over the years had expressed interest in re-naming the town, which by now had become the only center of population in a county that was as large as one or two of the smaller New England states taken individually.

Joe was finding his new existence exhilarating. Spring had arrived in the mountains. The accumulated winter snow had disappeared shortly before Joe's arrival, and the rains were becoming infrequent. His day began with an hour's fast-paced walk in the pine forest surrounding his cabin. This was followed by a simple breakfast of either cereal and fruit or bacon and eggs, the latter becoming more frequent as he improved his skill at cooking bacon into edible form while not overcooking the eggs. He then set to work for at least four hours. At first this latter activity consisted more of staring and pacing than it did writing, but recently the flitting mental glimpses of people and actions had begun to coalesce into a pursuable narrative, and he had begun to do more writing than pondering. In fact, he was becoming so engrossed in his work that his morning stint did not exhaust him mentally as it did initially. Joe's lunch was always followed by a second period of physical activity, after which he frequently returned to his computer for an hour or two of writing.

Late afternoon was reserved for his daily diversion of reading whatever paperback fiction that he had most recently bought at the grocery store in Craterville. This reading matter was not chosen recklessly. Whatever the genre of the book, he required something written with sufficient skill about plausible subject matter that it did not contrast too greatly with the small library of literary landmarks that he had brought with him. These he delved into regularly in the hope that he would profit from unconscious imitation. His daily pleasures regularly concluded with sitting on his porch to get a fresh look at his beautiful, unspoiled surroundings.

Joe had just sat down to begin his daily aesthetic inventory of his natural surroundings when he heard the approach of a vehicle up the two hundred yards of winding, unpaved lane that led from the paved road to his cabin. In fact, the vehicle turned out to be one that was familiar to all residents of the locale as the truck of the local man of all work, Evan Iverson. Joe had already come to regard Everson as the local treasure that he was universally accepted to be. He could repair or install almost anything. Failing that, he was candid about what he could not do but always seemed to be able to tell one where to turn for further assistance.

In all rural areas like Craterville and its environs, the male populace was uniform in only one characteristic. They had complete confidence that they knew how all the paraphernalia of contemporary life, from automobiles through septic systems, worked. Yet in the particular region of Craterville, the male population deferred to the superior knowledge, understanding and skill of Evan Iverson in dealing with the basic trappings of everyday life. Joe had already found that Iverson stories were the most often-repeated and enjoyed stories told in Craterville's sole gas station and the restaurant that relied primarily on resident rather than tourist business. The tales were always about a stranger, invariably portrayed as some urban vacationer, who challenged Evan Iverson's diagnosis of a mechanical problem and was soon brought to see the error of his inferior understanding.

Iverson's truck came to rest beside the porch of the cabin. Joe noted that the vehicle contrasted with the stereotypical conception of the work truck of the fabulously capable, self-employed handyman of American lore. That legend would require that the truck be ancient and spotted with innumerable dints and patches of rust but be always functional because of the near magical mechanical skill of its owner. The stereotype further required that the bed of the truck be piled with a jumble of tools from which the canny repairman alone could find just the right one to do the job at hand. In contrast, Everson's truck was no more than four years old and still sported its glossy dark blue paint free of dents or rust. The bed was bordered with three chromium cabinets, which those persons who had been privileged to see open knew to be packed with neatly arranged tools both manual and electrically powered. A rack extending over the length of the truck from the cab to the end of the bed carried ladders of several lengths as well as some lengthy tools for pruning, painting, prodding and whatnot.

The man who emerged from the truck was another violation of the traditional image of the all-purpose handyman. The six foot frame of the forty plus year old man still retained what could have been a young athlete's body. The weather-beaten face had not lost the vigor of youth. His brown eyes were penetrating, as though he could physically challenge whomever he faced but choose not to. Joe had never seen him without his black baseball-style cap that carried neither a sports nor corporate logo, as though to emphasize that the wearer carried no man's stamp. Whatever his most recent labors, his clothes gave no evidence of it. Nor was his garb the expected coveralls or bib overalls. A denim jacket was snug at both the well-muscled shoulders and the trim waist. His jeans were loose enough for ease of movement but neither baggy nor cut for style. Stout work shoes completed the picture of a workman whose appearance inspired confidence in his ability and intimidation of the manually unskilled.

Joe and Iverson knew one another because the owner of the cabin had arranged for Iverson to unlock the place and turn on the utilities when Joe arrived. "Joe," Iverson said as a greeting as he stepped on to the porch, "you got a problem?"

"Cabin's fine," Joe responded. "But I think that I need to have some tree trimming done." Joe stepped to the edge of the porch and pointed to where his car was parked in front of Iverson's truck. "I've got no place to park where the car isn't sure to get hit by pine cones, some almost the size of a football. or small branches falling off those pines. No major damage yet, but if we get a heavy wind, I could have a problem with a big branch falling on the car. How about trimming me a parking spot?"

Evan looked at Joe's car and upward at the trees branching over it. "Nice silver Beamer," he said smiling. "No point in letting that nice finish get nicked up. Shouldn't take more than two or three hours to clear a spot. I can do it next Monday for cash or tomorrow if you want me to bill you."

Joe smiled in surprise, not certain that he had understood Iverson's proposal. Today was Wednesday. It seemed illogical that the work could be done more immediately for delayed payment than for cash on performance. "I can do it either way, Evan, but I'm curious why it would be delayed a bit to have it done for cash."

Iverson smiled, "I forgot. You're new enough around here that you don't know my business system. I like to have enough money coming in each week to get by without debt. Other than that I like to have my time free. I've already taken in all the cash I want for this week. If I already had cash work scheduled for early next week or even farther beyond, I wouldn't be able to get to you for a while to do a cash job. But things have been slow and I don't have any cash work scheduled for next week. However, I can get a start on next week's income by taking a check tomorrow that I won't cash until next week.

"What if someone doesn't want to wait to pay cash?"

"They can get someone else. I have a list of other workmen I give folks if they need cash work fast. I have a copies of the list in the truck if you want it."

"No thanks," Joe was quick to say since he did not want to forego the services of the uniquely regarded local man, who, he now understood, was called Eventually Iverson by some local people. Out of mere curiosity, Joe asked, "What if someone doesn't want to be billed or insists on paying immediately for immediate service?"

"I just don't take the job. When I have the cash in hand that my weekly budget calls for, I'm done for the week. I'm happy to have my time be my own."

"So you don't take all the work you have time to handle? You got something against making extra money, Evan?" Joe asked with a mixture of disbelief and amusement.

"In a way," Evan responded as he returned Joe's smile. "Getting extra money would take up too much of my free time."

Joe decided not to continue this exploration of unconventional economics for fear the mere discussion of such aberration might bring on the demise of the established American work ethic, the fundamental premise of which is that after the fulfillment of one's needs is the point where real earning begins.

"I'll go for cash on Monday, I guess" Joe said, feeling a little like a game show contestant. "I'm trying to avoid debt. Keep life simple." He could not resist a chuckle, realizing that, with his scrupulous avoidance of debt, he was tampering as seriously with the American economic system as was Evan Iverson.

"Fine," smiled Iverson, "I'll be here first thing Monday morning around eight. If you're not already up, my power saw will get you up soon enough." With a salute-like wave, he got into his truck and quickly disappeared into the trees of the lane which wound back to the state road.

2

NORMALLY, JOE'S ONLY DEVIATION from his daily routine was his occasional trip into Craterville for groceries. To avoid guilt, Joe shopped for groceries after the day's writing effort had been completed. On the day after Iverson's visit, Joe needed a particularly inventive effort to come up with a minimally appealing lunch. Thus a trip to the market would be necessary if anything faintly resembling a decent evening meal could be expected. Joe decided to give himself a special treat. He would do his shopping late enough in the afternoon that he could have dinner in town and provide himself a day of relief from his as yet not fully-developed cooking skills.

At four-thirty in the afternoon Joe sat in his car where the lane from his cabin met the state road and waited for three logging trucks following closely on one another to pass so that he could turn onto the road into town. Each truck and its trailer unit carried five or six logs of more than thirty feet in length and three to four feet in diameter. The large imposing trucks and the huge logs they carried would be an intimidating presence to have following one on the two-lane state road. Joe was satisfied to wait until they were well on their way ahead of him as they rumbled their noisy way toward Craterville and through it down the road to the saw mill that was ten miles down the road from town.

He had driven most of the mile that brought him to the edge of town when he had to stop behind the caravan of trucks. The size of the loads ahead of him was each so high and wide that he could not see what was the reason for the delay. Drifting his car a few feet toward the center of the road to have a look around the trucks, he saw the stopped school bus with its red lights blinking and youngsters emerging from its door. Craterville's high school aged population was returning from their daily twenty mile trip each way to the sole high school in the area, which was in the neighboring city of Santa Clara in the county of the same name.

In a few minutes Joe was again trailing the logging trucks into the town of Craterville, the principal street of which, named for the Sutter of gold strike fame, consisted of two lines of commercial buildings strung for four blocks along each side of state route 110. The three streets which intersected each side of Sutter Street each ran for about a hundred yards before ending at the forest that surrounded Craterville. These side streets were lined with the homes of the town's one thousand residents. The buildings on Craterville's main street had not been modernized in a visible way since the town's founding in 1854. Several of the buildings, among them: the bank, a small hotel, and the town hall, were distinctive and attractive relics of a brief period of affluence when the founding of the town was prompted by a gold strike in the 1850's on the creek that ran just beyond the south edge of town and parallel to the state road. A number of non-descript buildings of the same vintage as the attractive structures that dated from the town's founding mingled with the few landmark buildings. These buildings were built as emporia to provide hardware, supplies and other essentials to mining and related enterprises. They remained in well-worn resemblance of their original state. Their merchandise changed as the town adjusted to the loss of its original reason for being and made itself useful to the tourists and vacationers who had become a necessary supplement to the logging and lumber milling industry that sustained the town now.

In his one month of residence, Joe had become sufficiently acclimated to circumstances in Craterville that he did not use one of the parking spaces on Sutter Street, into which local residents hoped tourists would find their way. He turned the corner at the town's only grocer store, which was housed in a two story building at the corner of Sutter Street and Second Street. The building's facade was no different than it had been at the construction date of 1855 that still showed at the top center of the side facing Sutter Street. In fact, the good condition of the wood frame building's gingerbread overhang of the sidewalk and its fresh paint showed the structure to be in better condition than some of the neighboring buildings devoted to small shops that counted mainly on the vacation trade for their existence. Joe parked in the ample lot behind the building housing the grocery and entered the store's rear entrance that was the usual path preferred by local residents.

The store remained the pleasant surprise it had been for Joe when he arrived a month ago. The variety and selection of frozen and canned foods was comparable to an urban market. The fresh meat and fowl choices were not as broad a selection as a major chain market, but the quality of cuts was as good as those to be found anywhere. There was no fresh fish, but there was a variety of frozen fish in the sizable freezer. Of course, Joe's limited cooking skills necessitated his favoring cold cuts, hamburger and sausages. He rarely summoned sufficient courage to tax his cooking abilities with cuts of meat, fish or poultry that would require complicated and careful preparation. Besides, he did not care to spend too much of his time preparing meals. On the other hand, he found it necessary to restrict his purchases of quickly-consumable snack foods, since he had long since recognized that for him the terms "a container" and "a serving" were synonyms.

Because the local hardware store limited its stock to only those tools and materials useful to skilled workmen and because the town lacked a bookstore, Joe was pleased that the Craterville Grocery retained the character of an old time general store. Beside the wide range of household gadgets was a section stocked with a considerable number and variety of paperback books ranging from classics to well-written popular fiction. Thorough examination of the selections enabled Joe to find the readable contemporary authors who were neither too facile nor superficial in their tales while exhibiting ample skill in their use of language. Rarely did he find a classic that he did not already have, but even in this category he occasionally found books that he had yet to read. He now acquainted himself with authors about whom he had developed an irrational prejudice on sampling them during his college days. Reading them now, Joe usually had the experience of wondering how he could have disliked the work of a writer that he now found not only meaningful and enjoyable but also admirable as well. Perhaps, he now mused, trying to write good fiction gave him a new respect for anyone who had done it well.

Since Joe always began his grocery shopping in the book section, it eventually became necessary to conclude his browsing and choose some books so that he could begin to fulfill his primary purpose in coming to the grocery store. Being more decisive in choosing food that in choosing books, Joe soon arrived at the register with a cart full of food and other essentials. He was a little disappointed to find that the register was not tended by the woman who managed the store but the young, high-school aged clerk who sometimes worked at the register. The pleasant Chinese-American lad was bright, efficient and accommodating, but he was not going examine Joe's reading choices as the manager always did and offer her assessment of his reading taste. She often had read what he had chosen and endorsed her favorites. She obviously was a voracious reader herself and continued her comments and questions about books until she completed bagging Joe's purchases. Joe enjoyed their brief dialogues and looked forward to them as a pleasant adjunct to his food-buying chore.

With the perishables stored in the cold chest that was now a fixture in his car trunk and the other bags wedged along side the chest to prevent their spilling, Joe closed the car trunk and walked the short distance to The Forty- Niner Diner. This unpretentious restaurant with its simple and pleasant interior had a special status with local residents, as Joe had quickly learned after arriving in the locale. Both local patrons and the servers in the Niner, as locals referred to the place, treated strangers respectfully but warily. Joe had been seen here often enough now that he sometimes received a nod of greeting from a fellow diner. The serving staff was near to treating him cordially. The quality of the food was as good or better than that to be found in the several touristy restaurants on Sutter Street, including the one in the local hotel, which touted itself as serving the most elegant cuisine in the region. The Niner did not strain at providing the same niceties of service and innovations in the menu that tourists would find on Sutter Street. However, the standard American fare was well-prepared from quality ingredients and no one left The Forty-Niner Diner regretting he had come.

There was more sprightliness than usual in the restaurant as Joe made his way to a vacant table and sat down. The dinner hour clientele of about a dozen people were all involved in the same dialogue, which had apparently produced some amused reaction just as Joe had entered and sat at a vacant table. Joe looked about him as the middle-aged waitress laid a menu and a glass of water before him and wordlessly turned from the table. Her silence was a sign of acceptance, Joe understood. The first few times he had been a customer, his server had greeted Joe as proper business etiquette demanded. For accepted members of the community, a welcome was more properly assumed rather than expressed. As the waitress returned to join the fringe of the energetic conversation, Joe looked at the group rather than the menu.

The woman he recognized as the manager of the grocery store was in the center of the group clustered at three tables in the rear of the room closest to the kitchen. The group was predominantly male, the only females being two waitresses and the grocery store manager. With the same animation that Joe enjoyed in the handsome woman's comments on books, she appeared to be in the middle of a lecture directed toward the men. The audience displayed a good-humored skepticism about what they were hearing but were nonetheless attentive and respectful to the speaker. The woman looked earnest but not overly intense. Joe could see her making a series of points by successively touching each finger of her palm upward right hand with the index finger of her left hand. The series of statements completed, she tapped a clipboard which lay on the table before her and offered a pen to her listeners. Joe surmised that she was seeking signatures for the sheet that was on the clipboard. However, none were forthcoming during the considerable pause that followed the completion of her appeal. Saying something else that produced a ripple of laughter from her listeners, the woman got to her feet and gestured resignedly.

She tucked her clipboard under her arm and appeared to be leaving the restaurant when she spotted Joe and started toward him. Smiling confidently as she stopped beside his chair, she asked, "May I speak to you for a minute?"

Joe looked up at the tall, willowy form, the fine-featured face, and the short, dark-brown hair waving to the back of her head. He reflected that these features were a good match for the radiant personality that she had shown in each of their brief conversations. Being careful not to exceed the limits of mountain courtesy toward women by getting to his feet, he pushed the chair to his right away from the table and invited her to sit.

Settling into the chair, she offered her hand and said, "My name is Carey Siebold; maybe you recognize me from the grocery store?" Joe nodded affirmatively. Carey smiled and placed her clipboard on the table. Her lustrous amber eyes focused on Joe earnestly. "I'm collecting signatures for a petition to the mayor and the town council asking them to pass an ordinance to prevent logging trucks from using Sutter Street, the state road through town. Will you sign it, please?" She slid the clipboard toward him and offered her pen.

"You didn't get any signatures back there," Joe said, nodding toward the tables from which she had come. "Why not?"

"They're afraid that people will lose jobs logging or at the sawmill if the trucks are prohibited from town," Carey said without hesitation.

"Sounds like a good reason not to sign," Joe reasoned.

"Jobs are not likely to be affected if we keep the trucks out of town," Carey said with a shake of her head. "There's another road, county road 5, from where they're cutting trees to the sawmill. They'll just have to go thirty miles farther." Joe saw that Carey could read the doubt he felt. The state road which was also the town's main street was the only road of any kind that he knew of through this sparsely populated, mountainous region. Carey formed a circle with her hands on the table. "True, the road through town is also the only road through the bowl of ridges we're sitting in. But there's also a road—just as good as the one through town—that circles around the bowl. It goes by the sawmill. I admit, it is thirty miles longer to get to the sawmill that way. But that's a small price to ask the lumber company to pay to preserve the quality of life and the tourist trade of this community. Believe me. The lumbering operation is much too lucrative to be abandoned just for having to truck the logs a bit farther."

"How come no one back there was convinced?" Joe asked, nodding toward the group from which Carey had just come.

"Even if the trucks have to use the long way, the lumbering business will stay," Carey repeated. "However, some local folks are speculating that anyone who is known to have signed or a relative of anyone who has signed might lose their job in the forest or at the mill in retaliation."

"Their union wouldn't protect them?" Joe inquired.

"Union?" Carey smiled. "You don't know loggers. Their opposition to unions is a bit more rabid than their employer's."

Joe looked at the clipboard. "You do have some signatures."

"Those are mostly merchants who think their business is being hurt and retirees who have nothing to lose and don't care for the noise and dirt from the trucks," Carey explained.

"No hardcore environmentalists?" Joe asked. He no sooner asked the question than he realized that he was not asking out of interest in the petition. He mainly wanted his conversation with Carey Siebold to continue. Her physical attractiveness had not escaped him in their brief conversations at the grocery. Nor had he previously been immune to the appeal of talking with her. This was his first chance to enjoy her company beyond the duration of a few sentences at the store register, and he wanted it to continue. He did not think that his desire to converse with the pretty, amiable woman was a matter of loneliness. He had not yet been long enough removed from the over-peopled context of his former work environment and its urban circumstances to be missing human contact. Quite the reverse; he was enjoying his isolation. Yet he wanted to continue his contact with this woman at the moment.

Joe was struggling for his next question when Carey said, "Actually, we're surprisingly short of hardcore environmentalists around here."

"What?" Joe reacted with surprise. He had been focused on her eyes rather than awaiting her response to his question.

"Hardcore environmentalists," Carey said, "You asked about them. Would you be one, by chance?" she asked hopefully.

"A supporter of the cause, not an activist," Joe said.

"Well, then," Carey smiled and offered her pen to him, "you should be adding your name to this petition, shouldn't you?"

Joe returned her smile but did not take the pen immediately. "I'll sign on one condition."

"Which is what?" Carey asked with look of suspicion.

"That my signing doesn't obligate me to participate in any sort of activity later. I've no desire to chain myself to a tree or lie in front of a truck."

Carey chuckled rather musically, Joe thought. She said, "Those things are a bit out of my line as well. But I hope that you'd be willing to attend the town council meeting for the presentation of the petition."

Joe nodded decisively. "No, I wouldn't."

Carey measured him with a look. "Surely you're not so timid that you wouldn't just sit in the audience?"

"I would hope not," Joe said, his grin preventing any show of defensiveness. "I'm guarding my time—and my freedom, I admit--rather jealously."

Carey showed her amusement. "You really do want to get away from it all, don't you?"

"Well, that was the idea behind my moving here," Joe admitted. He could see that her curiosity was aroused. He chose not to elaborate. He did not want to be thought either pretentious or extraordinary. He had not let anyone tease out of him his reason for settling in the area. As people had noted his being about longer than a typical vacationer, they had made gentle inquiry about the reason for his presence. He had evaded those questions and prepared to do so again, though those lustrous eyes were a temptation to reveal the entire story of one's life.

"O.K." Carey affirmed and offered her pen again, "signing doesn't commit you to another moment's expenditure of time. In addition, if you sign now, I'll maintain absolute silence at the check out in the store from now on and get you out faster."

Joe took the pen and pulled the clipboard toward him. "Let's not get extreme now. I like those chats at the check out. I'll only sign if they *do* continue."

"In that case, I guarantee it," Carey said. She stood as Joe signed the petition. When he had finished, Joe handed the pen and clipboard to Carey. After a glance at the clipboard, Carey said, "I appreciate it, Mr. Bell," and smiled broadly. As she walked toward the door, Joe almost got up to follow in the hopes of continuing their conversation. Then he realized that he had not yet even ordered dinner, let alone eaten it.

3

ON THE MONDAY AFTER Joe signed the truck ban petition, Evan Iverson arrived at eight in the morning as he had promised to trim the trees that branched over the spot where Joe regularly parked his car. Joe left his computer long enough to wave a greeting at Iverson and returned to his work. Fifteen minutes later, Joe succumbed to the curiosity aroused by the buzzing of the power saw and the sound of tree limbs falling to earth to go to the porch to examine the work in progress. Iverson was perched about thirty feet up in one of the tall pines near the cabin; a belt laden with tools and the now silent the power saw sagged from his waist. His body was leaning at a forty-five degree angle from the trunk. There was a safety belt around the tree trunk and his waist. Joe surmised that there were grippers on Iverson's shoes which prevented his sliding downward. Iverson fired up the power saw again and wielded it with apparent ease. Obviously he had the arm strength to extend the considerable weight of the saw the full length of his arm and control its cutting. Joe watched for a while, impressed by Iverson's skill and daring, especially when the workman moved out on a thick branch that was meant to remain to take off some smaller branches that could be a problem should a heavy wind snap them off. Eventually Joe had to scold himself back to his work and managed to stay at it somewhat distractedly for a half hour until he heard Iverson's knock on his screen door.

When Joe joined Iverson on the porch, the rugged-faced, fit-bodied workman said, "I think I took off everything that would likely be a problem, Joe." Pointing to the bed of his truck, which was stacked full of similar length cuts of three to six inch diameter pine branches, Iverson said, "I have most of what I cut off on the truck now. The small stuff over there," he continued as he motioned toward a pile of thickly-needled brush, "I'll get out of here this afternoon or tomorrow before it dries out and becomes a problem."

"Great, Evan," Joe nodded. "Let me get my wallet and we'll settle up. How about a beer to go along with the cash?"

"No, thanks, but some cold water would be great," Everson said cordially. Shortly, having settled payment for what Joe thought was a very reasonable amount, they were seated on the porch between the half-emptied pitcher of ice water Joe had brought out.

Joe leaned back and relaxed in his chair, enjoying anew the beautiful view of which he never tired, which was especially splendid on the sunny, mild day. "Beautiful place, isn't it, Evan?" Joe offered with satisfaction.

"None prettier," Iverson responded. "Damn shame people can't leave it alone."

Joe smiled at the rugged workman. "I'm thinking you might have signed a petition recently," he inferred.

"Yeh, I did," Iverson nodded. "Not that where the trucks go is the most important problem. It's clear cutting the forest that's the real damage." Joe was familiar with the term 'clear cutting.' It meant that a logging operation did not take just the mature trees that were suitable to be milled into lumber, but they also cut down every tree in the stand being logged because it was cheaper and faster to do so than to selectively take only the prime trees for making into lumber.

"Well, at least keeping the trucks out of town would prevent part of the damage to the life style around here. Maybe a peripheral environmental improvement will lead to major ones later," Joe offered.

Iverson smiled sardonically, "You don't really think the council is going to pass that ordinance, do you?"

"You think not?"

"The mayor, who happens to have a real estate business, is one of those guys who believes that what's good for business is good for everyone. He'll never vote for the ban, and he controls the council ninety-nine percent of the time," Iverson explained with finality.

"What about the argument that the truck ban will be good for the tourist business? Won't that sway the mayor?"

Iverson responded with a negative shake of his head. "Tourism's not the big money, Joe. For Mayor Sulliband, the truck ban's a matter of either backing a bunch of little pockets or one big, very deep pocket. The mayor is never confused about the close connection between money and power. You can bet he'll make the council see the issue as he does."

"How'd the mayor happen to get a council full of toadies?"

"Oh, no one around here considers them toadies. They're what passes for respected members of the community in Craterville," Iverson said while half-suppressing a chuckle. "All solid citizens, the four of them: a school principal, a minister, a hardware store owner—those three being the only person of their vocations in town—and one of the forest rangers. All four share a fixation with trying to avoid a vote that would annoy anyone, particularly anyone deemed important."

"Hard to believe they could get where they are in life without some backbone," Joe mused.

Iverson shook his head and showed his dismay. "The only goal Principal H. Lee Simpson has outside the school building is to be inoffensive. He runs a good primary school through the ninth grade. The kids do fine when they go off to the consolidated high school in Santa Clara. But, force him to take sides in a controversy and he's likely to faint dead away.

"The forest ranger, Brian Harrison, on the other hand, thinks his job compels him to be what he considers neutral. On the use of federal land, for example, he is simultaneously for preserving the forest, letting everyone use it responsibly, and not interfering with the Sierra Logging and Lumber Company doing what they please.

"Homer Jepson, the hardware store guy," Evan sighed dismissively, "is one of those small business owners who identifies with corporations. Like the mayor, he thinks what's good for business with a capital B is good for everyone.

"And finally there is the Reverend Billy Purefoy. I can't speak of him rationally. I'll just let you experience his simplistic, sloganeering, religiosity for yourself."

Joe smiled mirthlessly at Evan Iverson. "So I guess you wouldn't trouble yourself to attend the council meeting to sit through what you are convinced is an inevitable rejection of the petition."

"Oh no," chuckled Iverson as he got up to go. "I wouldn't miss it for the world. Better than anything TV has to offer."

4

INFLUENCED BY EVAN IVERSON'S adverse description of the Craterville town council and his prediction of the outcome of the request to ban logging trucks from the road through town, Joe changed his mind about not attending the council meeting. Besides, in addition to viewing what promised to be fascinating theatre, he would be acceding to Carey Siebold's request that he attend. She would be especially surprised at his presence because of their brief conversation several days ago.

As Carey was bagging his purchases the day before his dialogue with Evan, she had asked him if he had re-considered his refusal to attend the meeting. To his response that he had not, she adopted an elaborately exaggerated air of unconcern, saying how strange it was that some people who signed petitions felt no obligation to support their fellow petitioners. Joe was about to defend his commitment to non-involvement when the grin Carey could not suppress gave away that she was playing with him. With similar feigned seriousness, Joe told Carey that he would not be there physically but he would be with her in spirit. Carey pushed the cart with his bagged groceries at him and said with an air of melodramatic despair that she supposed that would have to do.

The evening of the meeting, he waited until the very last minute before its scheduled starting time before entering the chamber in the town hall in which the council met. Quickly surveying the audience space that occupied the two-thirds of the room closest to the wide doors through which one entered, Joe saw that there were only a few vacant spaces in the tiered benches of a seating area that looked sufficient to accommodate over a hundred people. He slipped into the partly unoccupied back row bench and began to examine the surroundings he was seeing for the first time.

The grandness of the room impressed him despite a few indications of neglect. The upholstery of the audience benches was faded and worn; however the benches themselves were made of beautifully finished carved oak. The same fine-grained wood had been used to panel the walls and construct the railing that separated the audience from the seating space for the council. Facing the public seating area was a lengthy counter built like a judge's bench behind which were five high-back leather chairs. This imposing separation also was made of oak. The beautifully carved wood showed a scene characteristic of the region's early settlement. Several miners stood in or crouched beside a stream as one man panned for gold. Joe concluded that the opulent appointments of the council chamber, like the town hall itself, which seemed disproportionately grand for the humble hamlet of present-day Craterville, were a remnant from the town's brief period of affluence during the gold mining era. The dwindling light of evening was still sufficient to let the stained glass windows behind the council dais show attractively. Here the scenes of the region's early settlement honored other aspects of endeavor than mining, being scenes of farming and lumbering. The total effect of the room was so pleasing that any person with even a minimal sense of history would hope for the building's preservation.

Though the scheduled time for the meeting had past by several minutes, the town council had yet to make an appearance. Joe knew Carey Siebold must be in the assemblage somewhere, but the crowd was large enough that it took him a moment to spot her. Leaning to his left, he saw a knot of people conferring at the left corner of the front of the public seating area. Their attention was focused on one person. It was no surprise to Joe that it was Carey Siebold to whom they listened and nodded. She looked like a coach giving her team last minute instructions. Joe observed again her handsome profile, the firm chin, the straight nose and the high cheek bones always ready to permit her cheeks to dimple into a smile. Her listeners returned Carey's smile as she chatted with them amiably. He was almost sorry that he had not agreed to accompany her to the meeting, if nothing else, for the pleasure of being near her. He knew that she was very serious about the problem of the truck traffic, and he hoped her efforts at having it re-routed would succeed. He wished he had been more emphatic in telling her so.

The room hushed suddenly as a door at one end of the dais opened and the five-member council filed in to occupy the seats behind the counter. Joe did not find them an impressive looking lot, though they radiated self-importance as they arrived at their places, each of which was indicated by a name plate, and seated themselves. The eyes of each surveyed the audience with a wary expression. Joe assumed that the public turnout for the meeting was more numerous than normal, and the councilors seemed unsure about what to make of the situation. The topic Carey and her fellow petitioners were raising could hardly be unexpected. The signature drive in the small community could not have left many townspeople in the dark about what the main feature of the evening's agenda would be.

Of the five person group of councilors, Joe could see from the nameplate of the man in the center that he was also the mayor. Apparently, as mayor, he chaired the council meetings, and he immediately proceeded to do so by tapping a gavel to quiet the room.

The mayor took the council through a sequence of preliminary matters and the disposition of several items of routine old business. The audience squirmed impatiently during this activity. It was obvious that they had only one reason for being here and were impatient for the matter to be addressed. Mayor Sulliband, as his nameplate identified him, announced the arrival of the portion of the meeting devoted to new business. He paused briefly before stating that a group of the town's residents had petitioned to be heard on a matter of concern to them. His four fellow councilors looked neither surprised nor pleased. Stating that he had asked the group to identify a spokesperson, he invited that person, whom he did not identify by name, to address the council.

Carey stood and positioned herself with the side wall of the chamber behind her so that she could face both the council and the audience. Her presentation was brief, well-organized and devoted to the issue. She began by saying that since logging had been initiated six months ago on a tract of forest east of town, the traffic on the state highway which was also Craterville's principal street had changed drastically. The numerous daily truckloads of logs through Craterville to the sawmill ten miles west of town were causing both an economic liability and damage to the quality of life in the community. Carey added that particularly on weekends, when the number of tourists was most numerous, Sutter Street had become both more congested and more hazardous, a situation which had already caused many potential visitors to bypass Craterville and seek the pleasures and purchases of their recreational time elsewhere among the mountain communities. Local merchants who depended on the tourist trade would confirm the fact that their sales had declined compared with the same period of the previous year. Of equal importance, Carey continued, was the hazardous effect that the passage of the trucks with their huge loads was having on driving situations through which local residents were having to maneuver. The lengthy vehicles and their huge loads over-burdened Craterville's main street as they would any street in the center of a town anywhere, notwithstanding Craterville's being in a small mountain community. Besides the increased danger from the presence of the trucks, the noise and dirt that they brought into the previously quiet and clean community had further damaged the quality of life in Craterville. She urged that the council not forget that peacefulness and a clean environment were reasons which had brought some of Craterville's residents to chose it as home in the first place. For all these reasons, Carey concluded, the three hundred and twenty-seven petitioners were asking the council to pass an ordinance prohibiting the logging trucks from passing through Craterville. To require the lumber company to absorb the minor cost and inconvenience of using a more circuitous route from the logging site to the saw mill was not too much to ask the lumber company to preserve the economy and environment of Craterville, Carey concluded.

After Carey sat down, Mayor Sulliband grinned coldly and said, "Before members of the council react to the petitioners' request, perhaps other persons in the audience might wish to comment." In the brief silence that followed the mayor's invitation, Joe studied the man. In the ethos of a small mountain town, where a sport coat and a button down shirt worn without a tie was the height of formality, the mayor wore a navy blue suit, a white shirt and red and blue striped tie. His round face looked robust rather than jowly and he was bald except for a close-cut fringe of hair from his temples around the back of his head. He looked sure of himself. Something about the expression on his face indicated that, if no one accepted his invitation to comment, he would be happier than if they did. Joe sensed that there was nothing of the 'good ole boy' about him. He guessed that Sulliband had not become mayor to enhance his status but to control the course of things.

After two almost timid statements were made by people who thought the ordnance prohibiting trucks was a good idea, opposition was expressed by a man who was a logger and feared for the employment of himself and a number of other men in town if an ordnance was passed that endangered the town's principal industry. He for one, would be glad to see the tourist industry diminish somewhat, he said, since he found the tourist traffic at the height of the summer season a greater nuisance than the logging trucks. This minimizing of the value of the tourist trade brought vigorous defenses of it by several merchants arguing two points. The first was that the economic impact of tourism was being underestimated by the previous speaker's remarks. The second was that the quality of life for residents in general and school age people in particular, whose only opportunities for summer employment were in the stores, would be greatly reduced if the stores that depended on tourist trade to remain viable disappeared.

The comments by persons in the audience began to get increasingly adversarial as people with a beneficial or damaging personal stake in the issue attacked people with opposing views rather than offering new arguments. With an august demeanor, the mayor stopped the comments from the audience and decreed that it was time for the council to begin its discussion.

As the four council members other than Mayor Sulliband made their remarks, Joe observed that Evan Iverson was mainly correct in his appraisal of their voting predilections. Jepson, the hardware store owner, stated forcefully that banning the logging trucks from Sutter street would be an infringement of the lumber company's right to conduct its business freely and that other businesses should not be seeking an advantage through regulation of someone else's business. The forest ranger Harrison and the school principal Sampson, as Iverson had predicted, saw justice in both the arguments for and against the ban and avoided indicating which were more persuasive. Reverend Purefoy gave a pietistic little sermon against conflict in general; therefore, he asserted, he would be guided by the position most strongly supported by his parishioners, although he did not indicate how he would know that preference. Joe had to stifle a gasp that an elected official would inject a partisan religious motivation into a civil issue; yet his astonishment was even greater when there was not a word of protest about what Reverend Purefoy had offered as a basis for his coming vote.

After the four had each spoken once, they silently declined the mayor's invitation to discuss the request for the truck ban further. He called for a vote. To Sulliband's directive that all councilors who supported the ordnance to ban logging trucks raise a hand, not one hand was raised. The mayor showed satisfaction in announcing, "The request for such an ordnance is defeated."

As a murmur began in the audience, Councilman Sampson said, "Point of order, Mr. Mayor, I think that we had better complete the formality of the vote. I would not be comfortable for the record to appear that we had all voted against the ban."

The mayor looked for a moment that he might disdain rigid observance of parliamentary process in the face of a foregone outcome. Then he said with a tinge of impatience, "Of course, we should preserve formality." With a glance in each direction at his colleagues, he requested, "All those opposed to the establishment of a truck ban ordnance indicate by raising your hand."

Only Jepson and Purefoy raised their hands. The mayor swiveled his head twice in each direction toward his colleagues in obvious surprise at the actual vote against the ordnance.

Sulliband looked non-plussed for a moment. Then he curtly requested, "Abstentions?" Both Sampson, the school principal, and Harrison, the forest ranger, raised their hands.

The buzz in the audience increased in volume as Mayor paused thoughtfully. He glanced around the room. The corners of his mouth turned up slightly with an expression that was more knowing than amused. "It seems," Sulliband said deliberately, "that we have a complex parliamentary situation. The request for the council to adopt an ordnance banning logging trucks from driving through Craterville has not been accepted. However, it has not been rejected by a majority at this stage of the voting procedures. In such instances, the chair of the council, which is, of course, my position, would cast the deciding vote.

"I will, as it is my responsibility, do so. But before I do, I want to give the matter some additional consideration. First of all, I want to ascertain from legal counsel whether or not the council has the right to establish the ordnance in question. Secondly, I am going to talk to the management of Sierra Lumber and discuss the possibility of their making some accommodation in this matter.

"Until I can do those things, I would like the council to adjourn and hold this matter in abeyance."

Carey Siebold popped up from her seat. "Mr. Mayor," she began with a tone that revealed some exasperation, "this seems an unnecessary delay. We considered the legality of the ordnance before we began our signature campaign and are convinced that it is within the council's powers. As to your second consideration, you have known this petition was coming for some time. You could have already explored the matter with the lumber company if it seemed relevant to you."

Sulliband looked at Carey coolly. "Despite your assurances about the legality of such an ordnance, which I am sure are made in good faith, its legality would have to be confirmed by the attorney in Santa Clara that the town retains in all such matters. Frankly, I haven't already done it because I didn't think that the matter would get this far." Sulliband smile wryly. "You've gotten a lot more signatures than I expected. For the same reason, I didn't think that negotiation with Sierra Lumber was necessary. Since the decision has fallen on my shoulders," he paused and glanced with disapproval at Harrison and Sampson, "as a consequence of the unexpected abstentions, I feel the need for the additional consideration this matter is due.

"I am not sure that the full consequences that could befall this town have been carefully enough considered." Sulliband looked around the council chamber calmly. What murmuring there was from the audience seemed to give him confidence. He turned to his colleagues on the council and asked, "Will the council give me a motion for adjournment?"

To Joe, it appeared that both the pair who had abstained and the two who voted against the truck ban looked equally anxious to have the session come to an end. The mayor quickly had a motion and a unanimous voice vote for adjournment.

The council quickly disappeared through the side door at the end of the dais through which they had entered. The audience began to leave in clusters, each engaged in comment and speculation about the meeting and its outcome. From the bits of conversation that Joe overheard, it was obvious that each group of discussants was composed of people with similar views on the truck ban. Persuasion, if ever it had been intended, was at an end. The only dialogue people were interested in, Joe recognized, was the reinforcement of their convictions. He was reminded of the ill-named "problem-solving" meetings at his old job. He smiled at his no longer being there to endure those frustrating experiences.

He was still seated and enjoying his pleasant reverie when he heard someone say, "The meeting couldn't have been as much fun as that smile on your face indicates." Joe looked up and saw Evan Iverson, whom he had not seen in the audience despite his cursory survey for familiar faces during the meeting.

"I was just enjoying my relief that I don't have to participate in meetings like this one any more," Joe explained.

"But they are a certain amount of fun if you aren't involved," Iverson offered.

"Yes," Joe agreed, "but this one didn't have much suspense for you. Your prediction shows a very accurate understanding of the inclinations of the councilors."

"They're pathetic, aren't they?" Iverson said with a disgusted shake of his head. "But I think that a couple of them surprised the mayor a little bit tonight."

"It's hard for the meek to know sometimes which way the wind is blowing," Joe said unsympathetically.

They were sharing their amusement when Carey Siebold approached the doorway with several of her fellow petitioners. She left her cohorts as they proceeded through the door and approached Iverson, who was standing behind the backmost bench, in which Joe was still seated. She squared before Iverson with one hand on a hip and said, "Well, I suppose you're feeling prescient. Your prediction came true." Carey looked resigned but not angry. Iverson smiled sympathetically. Joe had not known they were acquainted.

"I wasn't exactly right," Iverson mused. "I thought they would unanimously send the petition down in flames after a very brief discussion. I don't know why you pressed Sulliband to vote. He'd have made the majority against the truck ban tonight."

"If he's going to defeat it, why didn't he just do it now?" Carey wondered. "He's given us some time to work on more people."

Iverson made a cautioning gesture. "And himself more time to find a way to wriggle out from under. You know he loves to have his way without having to bear sole responsibility. A vote tonight would have put the decision squarely on his shoulders. He's given himself time to maneuver."

Carey looked determined. "And me time to work on the people." Carey looked from Iverson to Joe and back again. "I don't suppose I can count on either one of you two lumps for help?" Their silence gave her the answer to her question. She said, "I thought not." And walked out the door.

"Does my fellow lump want a cup of coffee?" Joe asked Iverson. "I'll buy."

Feeling chastised, they nonetheless headed toward the Niner Diner in good spirits.

5

THE RESIDENTS OF CRATERVILLE did not have long to wait before learning of Mayor Sulliband's decision in the matter of banning logging trucks from Sutter Street. Four days after the council meeting, the townspeople, including those outlying residents like Joe, received his decision by mail. He explained in his brief letter that he had ascertained from the town's attorney that, although Sutter Street was technically a state road, the rural circumstances allowed the flexibility that granted the city council the authority to establish a regulation such as the one that the petitioners had requested. He wrote that he subsequently discussed with The Sierra Logging and Milling Company what the impact on their operations in the area of Craterville would be if their trucks were prohibited the use of the road through Craterville. The company's management told him that the thirty miles of additional distance necessitated to use county route 5 to truck logs from the tree stand being cut east of Craterville to the saw mill west of town on state route 110 would slow operations to the extent that layoffs would be necessary both in the logging and milling operations. The company estimated that seventy-five jobs would be lost. The mayor stated that the effect of this loss of jobs, which would fall almost entirely on Craterville residents since the company's work force had few workers who commuted from any distance to the mill or the logging site, was obvious. Mayor Sulliband asserted that this blow to the town's economy would be more serious than the projected loss of tourist revenue. Hence, he stated, he was voting against the proposed ban on logging trucks. Thus by a vote of three opposed and two abstaining, the ban was rejected, he concluded.

Joe was not surprised at the outcome. He also noted that Evan Iverson had been correct that the mayor would find a way to deflect from himself any onus for the decision, which would be unpopular with the petitioners, who were a sizable percentage of the town's voting population in local elections. Joe mused wryly that no one could quarrel with a decision to protect jobs. Besides, since Sierra Logging could operate with any size labor force that it pleased, who could say that the threat of layoffs was merely a tactic? Although Joe knew nothing about the lumbering industry, he could nevertheless reason that, by stockpiling a durable material like logs, the rate of cutting trees and milling logs was not necessarily governed by rate of moving the logs from the forest to the mill. However, the company could no doubt use the added distance as a rationale for changing the pace of operation if it wished. Joe concluded with dismay that the harsh realities of power had been shown once again to be insuperable, even in a society where the mass of people had a voice.

That afternoon, Joe went to the Craterville Grocery in search of cleaning supplies, a sort of materials Joe tried to avoid overstocking for fear of encouraging overly frequent use. He expected to find Carey Siebold either angry or depressed as a result of Mayor Sulliband's decision on the logging truck ban. Surprisingly, he found her to be her usual pleasant self as he approached the check out with his carefully limited purchases of cleaning materials. To her smile and warm greeting, Joe responded, "You're in very good spirits for someone who just had her labored-over project shot down by the mayor. "

"You think that battle's over?" Carey grinned, "Far from it."

"Now what?" Joe hazarded in view of her mood. "You going to run for town council? Or maybe mayor?"

With feigned seriousness, Carey said, "Actually, you're my candidate for mayor, but I wasn't going to bring it up yet."

"That's horrifying, even in jest," Joe responded with a shuddering of his shoulders that underscored his distaste.

Carey chuckled, "I've seen people who had a close call with a bear look less frightened. Relax. We have something less divisive in mind than political action. Facts are what are called for," she said, playing at a politician's tone of seriousness for a moment. Continuing seriously, she said, "We're organizing to monitor the number of trucks that pass through town to get an accurate daily average of the number of trips. Then we'll see if that number of trips could be made during a day using the longer route, county 5. We're betting that the data will show that the facts won't support the assertion that the longer route requires a slow down of operations and thus layoffs."

"I'm impressed with your group's strategy; however, you don't really think applying facts to an obviously political decision ever makes a difference, do you?"

"Oh, my," Carey loudly inhaled audibly and showed an exaggerated wide-eyed expression. "Listen to the poor, cynical man!"

Joe smiled. "I prefer 'realist'."

"So does every other cynic in the world," Carey countered. "Why don't you do something for the nourishment of your soul. Help us out."

Joe frowned and struggled for an answer. It was hard to say 'no' to so charming a woman. "Actually," Carey continued before

Joe had formed his answer, "I was selfishly thinking of a way you could help me."

"I'm listening," Joe responded as coolly as he could, not to seem too interested in what now appeared as an attractive possibility.

"We're trying to get several people to separately clock the longer route from the logging site to the mill at the speed that the loaded trucks would travel. I volunteered to do a run, but my car's in uncertain condition at the moment. If you'd drive me in your car on my run, I'd be grateful."

"Does the task include lunch when the job's done," Joe asked

"Oh, absolutely," Carey agreed.

"Then you're on," Joe said as he as he picked up the purchases, which had been paid for and bagged as they had talked. "When do you want to go?"

"Day after tomorrow. Pick me up here at ten?" Carey asked.

"See you then," Joe agreed. It was a half-hour later that he was forced to admit to himself that he had violated his resolve to avoid involvements that would stand in the way of devoting his time to writing.

Two days later, when Joe drove up to where Carey waited at the back entrance to the grocery, he had long since rationalized that a single day's deviation from his normal writing routine did not jeopardize his commitment but was a brief diversion that would stimulate his writing when he returned to his task. As the trim figure of Carey, looking casual but attractive in a short tan leather jacket and tailored black pants approached the car, Joe was doubly convinced that his brief truancy was no mistake. As Carey got into the seat beside him, her greeting was accompanied with a smile. Joe appreciated once again how pretty Carey was without the use of make up. He admitted that there appeared to be a bit makeup around the eyes, but that understated emphasis added to the arresting quality of her eyes. Joe recalled that he had once seen an amber pendant the same shade of brown as those eyes, but of course, the hardened resin, with its entrapped insects, was less clear and pretty than Carey's eyes.

He returned Carey's greeting and suppressed a compliment about her appearance. Attributing his silence to wise circumspection, he told Carey she would have to direct him to the starting point of the journey for which they were to determine the driving time. Carey directed him eastward on Sutter Street where the road became state road 110 running east from town. Carey explained that the current logging operation was about twelve miles east of Craterville and near the barrier where the road ended below the loftiest ridges of the Sierra. Since they were not yet to the route to be timed Joe drove at his own unhurried pace, enjoying the forest and the occasional glimpses of the stream that ran along side the road. At this time in the spring, it still had enough flow from the last of the winter snow runoff to sparkle where the sunlight hit the water as it tumbled over its rocky bed. To Joe's comment on its beauty, Carey responded with the practical information that the stream, known as the south fork of the Miwok River, also fed the wells that supplied Craterville's water. Joe chided Carey for her practical mood amidst the surrounding natural splendor. Carey responded that Joe had not lived in the mountains long enough to have an awareness of the practical concerns of fire, drought and severe winter storms.

Their amiable small talk continued until they reached the point where it was obvious from the mud caked on the road that they were approaching the place where the logging trucks left the cutting area of the forest and turned on to the paved state road toward the sawmill to the west of Craterville. Joe made the u-turn back toward Craterville and decreased his speed to the range of 20 to 25 miles per hour as Carey directed. Some friendly loggers had informed Carey's group that the speed Joe now held to would be a fair approximation of the rate at which a loaded log truck would travel on the constantly curved two-lane road. The speed required careful monitoring on Joe's part since it was slower than even a cautiously driven car would travel. Carey jotted the time in her notepad as they had begun their run.

Joe lapsed into silence as he concentrated on his driving. Even though the curvy two-lane had not encouraged much speed on their trip back west, Joe had to resist the tendency to speed up beyond the supposed truck speed. They had traveled half the distance back toward Craterville when Carey pointed out again to Joe the turn on to county road 5, which was cut into the outside of the semi-circle of ridges which enclosed the west side of Craterville. Joe had no previous experience with this road that the log truck ban petitioners wanted the logging trucks to use; however, he concluded in about fifteen minutes driving county road 5 that it was in width, condition of the surface and contour similar to state road 110 that ran through Craterville. If county 5 continued throughout its length in the form and condition that Joe had found it in so far, it posed no more of a driving challenge to a log truck driver than did the direct route to the mill, despite being thirty miles longer.

Joe's having to focus on keeping his speed down not only kept conversation to a minimum, he was unable to permit himself more than momentary glances at his stunningly beautiful surroundings. This road, like the one through Craterville and on westward, sloped gradually downward to a lower elevation. However, rather than being bounded by ridges on both sides as was route 110 as it dropped to lower elevation, this road clung to one side of the ridges that surrounded Craterville. Beyond its outer edge was a precipitous drop into a deep chasm. From that unseen low point, another ridge of mountains jutted just as precipitously upward as the one to which the road Joe was traveling clung. Between watching his speed and controlling his car around the endless succession of curves, he was not able to enjoy the panorama of forest and rocky promontories. In fact it was a relief when they completed their semicircle around the Craterville ridges and rejoined state road 110 that came directly down through Craterville to the Sierra Logging Company sawmill and beyond. Joe held his leisurely speed for just five more miles on Route 110 and the sawmill appeared on his right.

He pulled off the road beside the road entering the sawmill and said, "Our run is officially over, right?"

Carey finished writing the time in her notepad, "It's over until we time the trip back," she said.

"You mean we're not going back the short way?" he asked with a trace of whine in his voice.

Carey explained patiently, "If we time the run back on county 5 and compute an average, we'll have a more accurate figure for the time the trip takes. Anyway, your pretend truck will be unloaded on the trip back, I'll let you hit as high as thirty or thirty-five on the way back."

"Right," Joe grumbled. "At thirty-five miles an hour on some of those curves, we'll end up several thousand feet straight down. I haven't mentioned how much I dislike driving mountain roads that drop off into space on one side and don't even have a guardrail, have I?"

Carey smiled, "Oh, you'll be fine after a good lunch."

"We're not having lunch back at the Niner?"

"I thought you deserved something a little special for helping me out, I got Mrs. Tejada, who can usually give me only two hours a day, to tend the store all afternoon. Let me do this. I'm rarely free to provide a thank you in the form of a mid-day meal," Carey offered soothingly. "Just about ten more miles down the road in Santa Clara, there's an Italian place which is awfully good--if you like Italian." Carey offered.

"Not a chain restaurant?" Joe asked suspiciously.

"Would I kid you?" Carey asked.

Joe offered his companion an askance look and said, "At this point, I'd best not answer that." He soon had them back on the road headed for Santa Clara.

The restaurant proved to be a delicious dining experience despite Joe's trepidation on entering the premises. The red and white checked tablecloths with centerpieces of partially melted candles which had run down over their wine-bottle holders made him suspicious. The murals depicting stereotypical Italian rural scenes increased rather than eliminated his doubts. He had had too many experiences where this type of appearance in an Italian restaurant substituted for flavor and authenticity in the food. This time the décor did not presage a disappointment in the food. From the miniature pizza wedges he chose as an appetizer, through the green salad of endive and artichoke hearts with a balsamic vinegar and olive oil dressing, followed by his meat ravioli entrée, everything was a flavorful perfection of the simple peasant fare that was the southern Italian menu.

As they waited for the dessert: zabaglione for two, which required some special preparation time, Carey said with an expression of vindication, "Well, did I not say you would be pleased?"

"If the zabaglione is up to the standard of the rest of it, I will admit that the city of Santa Clara does, indeed, have a first rate Italian restaurant," Joe responded with the amiability of the well fed.

The wait for dessert lapsed into a modicum of tension. The ride from Craterville had not permitted relaxed small talk. Their hearty appetites over a rather late lunch had restricted conversation as well. Now they found themselves, acquaintances for several months but largely strangers to one another, at close quarters with no choices but silence and finding some innocuous topic of conversation. Joe's usual strategy in such situations was to ask mundane questions about the other person. He had learned that most people's favorite subject was themselves. Besides, Joe's innate curiosity about people was one of the things that attracted him to writing fiction. Even more important than both factors was the reality that he was more interested in Carey than he had been in anyone else since he had left the corporate world for his rustic and somewhat isolated life.

Joe was rather sure his object in wanting to know more about Carey was not romance but getting to know an intellectually interesting person, not that he was immune to her attractive appearance. It was only the slightest of exaggerations to call her beautiful. Besides, two even more appealing qualities than her beauty were her maturity and the spirit of independence she radiated in totally unaffected fashion. Joe could easily imagine Carey as a senior corporate executive although she fit just as suitably as the owner and manager of a rural grocery store. In the spirit of learning something of her history, he sought answers about her background that were informative but not overly personal. Carey answered each question briefly but seemed more interested in following her answers with a question of her own as a means to acquire similar or even more specific information from him.

Carey smiled broadly after prodding out of Joe the reason for his residence in Craterville. "Chucked it all to take a shot at writing, huh?" Carey nodded. "I'm impressed--and wish you luck. It's a hard go, from everything I've heard and read. All that bridge burning is gutsy. I figured you for a bold one, though."

"You did, huh?" Joe said, his smile showed his pleasure at her assessment.

"Yeh, but I was thinking more along the lines of a bank robber on the lam," Carey said, feeling the need to change the mood and putting the moment of seriousness behind her.

"How else could I afford my luxurious life style," Joe countered. Then unwilling to give up the serious conversation, he asked, "What's your story? How did you come to run a grocery in the mountain village of Craterville?"

The dessert arrived during the brief interlude during which Carey seemed to be struggling to phrase her answer. She intently watched as the waiter spooned a serving of cherries and the rich vanilla pudding into a dish for each of them. She maintained her silence and lifted a partial spoonful of the pudding to her mouth. She murmured with pleasure to find the taste touched with an agreeably flavored liqueur. She showed further delight when her second spoonful turned up one of the sweet, dark cherries submerged within the pudding. Carey expressed her enjoyment of the flavorful combination and added her puzzlement that she had not discovered zabaglione before. Joe opined that she must not take too seriously the stipulation in the menu that it was only prepared for two. Joe stated without guilt that he had no qualms about ordering it for two when he ate alone. Carey chuckled agreeably at his admission of excess, though she accused him of indulging in a glutinous side of masculine behavior.

Joe paused between spoonfuls of his dessert and reminded Carey, "You never answered my question about how you chose to become Craterville's sole grocer."

Carey set down her spoon and began her answer with great deliberateness. "I was a corporate animal, just like you. I was vice president for purchasing and inventory for Better Quality Markets, one of the bigger grocery chains in the state. After a while it wasn't much fun. Since I knew how a mom-and-pop type market can beat the problem of not being a volume buyer which gets the price break that chains get from producers, I opted for a sane existence at something that I knew and could make work."

"No man in the picture at the time that you decided on the big change?" Joe asked, hazarding a question that might cause Carey to drop the subject.

"Ah, well," Carey sighed with resignation rather than anguish, "there was a guy. We agreed to disagree. The less said about it the better." With that, Carey returned to her dessert and Joe knew the subject was beyond further inquiry.

As they began the drive back to Craterville the long way around, Joe felt that he and Carey had become friends. He now saw her commitment to the truck ban effort as the current instance in an approach to living that insisted that life ought to be fair. He sensed that Carey believed that the impossibly of making life fair universally should not deter one from making it so to what small extent one could. Carey was neither a crank nor person on a selfish crusade. She was an admirable person of conscience. In short, he respected her. That was a basis for friendship rather than romance. Joe affirmed anew on his decision that romance did not fit into the life he led now. Friendship decidedly did. Hence, there was no reason for caution in his feelings about this woman of quality.

6

AS DID THE OTHER residents of Craterville, Joe soon saw the results of the research by Carey's group into the assertion that Sierra Logging had made to Mayor Sulliband. The company had stated that changing the routing of logging trucks would require layoffs in their operation. However, a week of careful monitoring by the truck ban group established otherwise. At the current volume of truck traffic studied over one six-day work-week, the group's findings, which were communicated in a letter to every household in Craterville, were that the use of county route 5 for a typical length work day rather than using the more direct state route 110 would at most result in one fewer truck load of logs per day reaching the sawmill.

This change, which was conceivably avoidable, showed that banning trucks from passage through Craterville should not force layoffs in the logging company's operation. The mailing ending with an urging to Mayor Sulliband to use the results of the research to engage in further negotiation with Sierra Logging about their voluntarily submitting to the truck ban through town. Joe was tempted to make an immediate trip into town to congratulate Carey on the effectiveness of this new tactic in her group's campaign.

However, he restrained himself. Having taken a single day's respite from his writing had not provided the basis for renewed energy as he had rationalized. Not writing on the day of his drive with Carey was the first such interruption of his work in weeks. He was like an alcoholic who had broken a sobriety pledge just once. Through several fretful days of managing only a paragraph each day, each of which proved on review of doubtful relevance to his story, Joe failed to return to his former level of productivity, a quantity of output which in Joe's case was never voluminous under the best of circumstances. He put in a week of longer than usual hours to get back to what he had come to think of as his normal output.

Thus it was almost two weeks after his trip with Carey that Joe drove into town to end his period of long hours of work and simple meals from his badly diminished supplies of staple and frozen food. To his surprise when he arrived at 3:00 p.m., the grocery store was closed. A sign in the window said that for the foreseeable future the store would be open from 12:00 noon to 2:00 p.m. and 4:30 to 6:00 p.m. Monday through Friday and all day Saturday from 8:00 a.m. to 6:00 p.m. Wondering what was the cause of this change from the usual 8:00 a.m. to 6:00 p.m. hours, Joe decided to get a cup of coffee at the Niner and see if anyone knew.

As Joe sat down at a table in the largely empty restaurant the waitress Joe knew from her nametag that said that she was Harriet brought him a cup of coffee without being asked. Joe thanked her and asked her if she knew why Carey was having such limited hours at the grocery store. The waitress expressed surprise that Joe did not know the reason. "She's been in the hospital in Santa Clara with a twisted knee and a cracked bone in the ankle of the same leg for three days now. Mrs. Tejada and Jimmy Chin are keeping the place open during the hours they usually fill in for Carey."

"How bad is it?" Joe asked, "What happened?" His desire to know overstepping the logic of asking questions one at a time.

The waitress sighed sympathetically, "Pretty bad injury to both joints, from what I hear. But she's coming along O.K., they say."

"How did it happen?" Joe asked again.

"The details aren't very clear," the waitress reported. "She fell while she and Grace Dawson were planting flowers."

Joe was uncertain that he heard correctly. His expression showed it, and his informant was prompted to continue. "You know that little circle between the two lanes of the road just when it leaves town at the west end?"

Since he lived east of town and rarely had reason to go to Santa Clara, Joe did not often drive west through Craterville; however he knew the little circle in the roadway and the large boulder of serpentine rock which sat in its center. He nodded his understanding so that the report would continue. "Carey and Grace were planting flowers in the circle—it's something a group of local ladies do every spring and tend throughout the summer. While they were working, Carey fell and twisted her leg."

"Strange," Joe mused, "she doesn't seem like the awkward type."

"Of course," Harriet with a conspiratorial look, "some people don't think that awkwardness had anything to do with it."

"What do you mean?"

"There were logging trucks passing on both sides of the circle when Carey when down," Harriet said. She looked as though the information spoke for itself.

"Good God," Joe gasped. "A truck knocked her down?"

"She says not, and from what I hear, she's not bruised."

"What's the woman say who was working with her?" Joe asked.

"She didn't see anything. She was planting at the base of the monument and had her back to Carey. Carey was working on the border bed around the edge of the circle."

Joe could see that it was a plausible inference that a truck had passed so close to Carey that she fell awkwardly trying to distance herself from the huge truck. "Damn," Joe grumbled and frowned. "Talk about being in the wrong place at the wrong time," Joe nodded sympathetically.

"Or the right place at the right time, from some people's point of view," Harriet offered knowingly.

"Surely no one thinks the truck intentionally crowded her?" Joe frowned.

"Carey isn't exactly Sierra Logging's favorite person, is she?" Harriet asked rhetorically.

"Why would anyone who's against the truck ban do anything so crazy? They've already won in the city council."

Harriet smiled wryly. "But it's not over, is it? And everyone knows who the leader of the protest group is, don't they?" Pausing as though she had made the conclusive point, Harriet arched her eyebrows and studied Joe. "You going to order anything?' she asked.

"No, just the coffee," Joe responded. As Harriet turned to go, Joe asked, "You know if Carey's allowed visitors?"

"Since yesterday," Harriet said as she stepped toward the kitchen. Joe took a swallow of the coffee, dropped a couple dollars on the table and headed for his car. He wanted to see for himself how Carey was doing. Since he had helped her continue her campaign against the logging company, he felt some responsibility for her injury. That reasoning seemed a little far-fetched even as it occurred to him, However, it would do as a rationale if Carey or any of her other visitors wanted a reason for his coming to the hospital.

As he drove west on Sutter Street out of Craterville, it occurred to Joe that he had never looked closely at the circle on the west edge of town or the boulder which was at its center. He was suddenly curious enough that he decided to familiarize himself with the place. When he neared the circle, he took care to pull completely off the right side of the road to park. Carey's accident made him more conscious of the possibility of a glancing collision with a logging truck. The circle was a mowed grassy area about thirty feet in diameter which separated the lanes of the road in either direction for an elliptical distance of about a hundred feet. The circle inside the ellipse was clearly identifiable by its flowered border and the six feet tall green serpentine rock with a bronze plaque in the center of another flower bed at the center of the circle.

Exiting his car, he crossed the westbound lane of route 110 and stepped over the foot wide ring of turned earth about three feet from the outer edge of the grass circle. Except for about six feet of snapdragons boldly showing their colors, the border ring was unplanted. Obviously Carey's accident had occurred when she had barely begun her task. Joe approached the boulder which was the eye-catching center of the circle. The naturally occurring trapezoidal shape sat with its larger end down, Even with part of it embedded in the ground, the stone was large enough that a driver could not fail to see it as he approached. A bed of red, white and blue petunias encircled the huge rock. The serpentine stone was a dark green color with spots of glossy surface that suggested polishing but were instead the natural state of the stone. The impressive boulder had a bronze plaque with raised lettering attached to its side.

The wording of the plaque paid tribute to the small detachment of union soldiers led by Captain Horace Broadbent who discovered gold in the nearby Miwok River in 1861. When a number of civilian miners arrived, the strike became a thriving mining operation that grew into the town of Craterville. Broadbent and his men, augmented by a faction of the miners, fended off the attempt by an equal-sized group of confederate sympathizers to ship the area's gold output to the rebel states. They provided the gold to the union authorities in San Francisco. Of course, Joe knew that Craterville had been a gold mining boom town for an approximate thirty year period beginning in 1861, but he had no previous knowledge of a civil war conflict having occurred in the region. He mused over the information on the bronze plaque attached to the green serpentine for a few minutes. Suddenly, he was startled by the roar of an approaching logging truck, which neared at a considerable speed since it was returning unloaded from the sawmill to the west toward the logging area east of town. He thought of Carey's accident while the truck roared by. No doubt the mere size and noise of the vehicle, let alone its passage close by, would be unnerving to someone standing near the edge of the circle. With a memory of the sound and sight of the truck firmly in mind, he returned to his car to proceed to Santa Clara for his visit with Carey.

7

THE RECEPTIONIST AT THE front desk of the hospital in Santa Clara told Joe that Carey had but one visitor with her at present, so he could proceed to her room if he wished. He waited for the elevator and wondered for the first time if he had made a mistake in coming. He hoped that Carey would not infer that a romantic interest in her had motivated his visit. The elevator arrived and opened to reveal a nattily-dressed Evan Iverson standing inside. The pressed navy blazer, gray, sharply-creased slacks and a button-down, pale blue, open-collared shirt were a drastic contrast from his usual denim attire. Joe greeted Iverson, who stepped off the elevator looking chagrined. "You headed up to see Carey?" Iverson asked with a tone that seemed to impart a warning.

"Yes," Joe affirmed. "How's she doing?"

"Oh, physically, she's getting on fine," Everson grumbled. "Mentally, the woman's lost all sense of reality."

Joe did not know how to interpret Iverson's statement, so he stood silently waiting for elaboration from the other man. Iverson looked frustrated. "She absolutely refuses to consider that there is something suspicious about her so-called accident," he said with the tone of someone reporting the incomprehensible.

"You think there was?" Joe asked.

"Well, Joe, how much of a believer in coincidence are you? Trucks passing in both directions at that exact spot at the exact time when the biggest thorn in the side of the logging company is gardening three of four feet off the edge of the paved road? If you think that's coincidence, then you believe that Jack Ruby just stopped by the Dallas jail for a cup of coffee and accidentally discharged a gun in the direction of Lee Harvey Oswald."

"Does Carey say the truck made a deliberate move to crowd her?" Joe asked.

Iverson waved his arms in frustration, "She says I have an over-active imagination."

"Do you?"

"For years, Joe, that woman's consistently accused me of having no imagination at all," Iverson snorted as he walked away.

Minutes later, Joe entered Carey's room. She was sitting up in bed reading. Her left leg was encased in an inflated cast from her hip to her toes. She looked up when she heard him enter and smiled. She put down her book face down on her lap and said, "I don't suppose you stopped by the Italian restaurant to get something for me to eat?"

"I'm afraid not," Joe admitted as he eased into the chair beside her bed. "That was thoughtless of me. Of course, you could have called me. I didn't even know about your accident, if that's what it was."

Carey looked at him askance. "You ran into that idiot Evan Iverson on your way in."

"You don't think that there could be something to his interpretation of what happened?" Joe asked calmly.

"I'm guessing that he didn't tell you my version of the accident." Joe shook his head negatively and Carey continued. "I was working on the border flower bed when I heard the trucks approaching at some distance. I was standing on the outside of the bed, so I decided to step inside the bed for safety's sake. As I turned and stepped over the bed, my left foot caught on something, probably a clod of dirt, and my right foot slipped on the grass, I went down with a twist on my left side. A bone in my left ankle cracked and the ligaments in my left knee got badly strained.

"That's all there is to it. I didn't step over the flower bed at the moment I did because a truck was bearing down on me. When I turned to step across the bed, I was looking down at the flowers I'd planted. I don't even know how near or far away the truck was. I wasn't concerned about it."

Joe was surprised at the clarity of Carey's recollection of the event in view of the severity of her injury, "You're sure you didn't glance at a dangerously close truck at all? Maybe your getting hurt pushed what you saw at that moment to the back of your mind," Joe asked.

Carey shook her head and grinned slightly "I wasn't traumatized by a narrow escape." She continued calmly, "I remember that I'd already started to step across the bed before I saw a truck. I wouldn't have known if the truck swerved toward me--or away, for that matter."

Joe recollected the strength of Evan Iverson's conviction. "You don't think the logging company or some driver loyal to the company is annoyed enough with you to try something drastic."

Carey gestured with one hand dismissively. "With the mayor and the town council in its pocket, why would the company bother?"

"How about a truck driver independently exercising his own annoyance? Just trying to throw a little scare into you?" Joe offered.

"Joe, that's both unlikely and irrelevant. I tripped. It's as simple as that."

"You've sold me," Joe shrugged. "I hope you're right, but Evan's speculation is thought-provoking, to say the least."

"Well, don't let Evan Iverson convince you of anything," Carey advised emphatically.

"I didn't realize he was so protective of you."

"It comes and goes," Carey responded with a bit of irritation. "Too bad it doesn't take the form of helping me when I need it."

"Something I can help with?" Joe offered.

"Jimmy Chinn was supposed to open the store all day Saturday for me. Saturday's when most local people stock up for the week, not to mention there being the weekend tourists. Now it turns out that Jimmy's unavailable. He's quite a track star, you know. His performance in a meet today qualified him for district competition which could qualify him for the state meet. Jimmy's offered to skip the meet and mind the store on Saturday, but there's no way I'd let him do that. He's worked so hard, and he's too good to pass up this chance."

Joe nodded. "I know Saturday's a busy day at the store. I went once and decided I'd stick to weekday shopping from then on."

Carey smiled wryly. "I'm almost glad Mrs. Tejada's not available for her usual two hours. Can you imagine what everyone's squeezing their shopping into two hours would be like for her?"

"Probably like those supermarkets you worked for on the day before Christmas," Joe suggested.

Carey let a laugh escape her. "That sounds like experience gained from a bachelor's approach to holidays."

"Why don't I open for you on Saturday? Regular hours." Joe offered.

Carey shook her head in refusal. "No. I know you have a routine, and I now understand how important it is that you stick with it."

"I can adjust my writing stint around the usual store hours," Joe explained.

"Your usual writing hours are just as important as the usual store hours. Certainly more important than Evan Iverson's septic tank job on Saturday," Carey said firmly. Then her face broadened into a smile and she looked over Joe's head. "And that's no - -."

In the pause, Joe grasped the word on which Carey had balked. "Oh, stop resisting and give in to it," Joe chided her.

"What?" Carey asked, still maintaining her smile.

"You were going to say 'and that's no crap.'"

"No exactly," Carey admitted. "But close enough."

"Being in this place is obviously rotting your brain," Joe jested. "When are you getting out?"

"They want to immobilize the leg for a while. I get a screw in my ankle and a hard cast from my toes to my thigh tomorrow. Then I have to stay a while and see if the leg looks to be mending right. The knee problem may delay my leaving too. They just won't say how long it's going to be. I hope not long. I've got to get back to work."

Joe thought seriously. "It's obvious that the store's got to be open the next couple Saturdays at least if famine is to be avoided in Craterville," Joe reasoned. "Let me open for you this Saturday and next Saturday if Jimmy Chinn can't. I won't skim the till. I promise."

"I'm mightily tempted to accept your offer," Carey admitted.

"You should give in to temptation occasionally."

"I doubt we're talking about the same temptation," Carey said.

"In this instance solely," Joe admitted.

Carey thought for a minute. "You think you could get the key from Jimmy?"

Joe rolled his eyes and said, "No doubt he'll be hard to find in a big city like Craterville, but I think I can handle it."

Carey narrowed her eyes and looked at Joe appraisingly. "If you're going to work for me, you're going to have to cut out that smart mouth."

"You're the one who'd better be careful or everything in the store's selling at two for the price of one this Saturday," Joe threatened.

"Oh, God, what have I done?" Carey groaned with feigned despair.

"You'll have a full report on Sunday," Joe said as he got up to leave.

"Do you even know how to work a cash register?" Carey wondered.

"It wasn't covered in graduate school," Joe said over his shoulder at the doorway, "but maybe Jimmy or Mrs. Tejada can do an all-nighter and give me just the basics." He disappeared from Carey's view as she groaned in mock despair.

8

THE BIGGEST PROBLEMS JOE had in being a store keeper that Saturday were not those he anticipated. He expected difficulty in locating various products for customers and dealing with transactions at the register. In fact, long time Craterville residents knew the location of the store's inventory better than he did and arrived unassisted at the register with their shopping lists complete. With the register's capability to identify prices and make calculations, Joe was left with little to do beyond making change or collecting credit card bills. The customers, grateful that the store was open at all and wanting to spare their volunteer storekeeper, bagged their own purchases before Joe could finish the financial part of the purchase.

His first major problem occurred before he even got to open the store. Half way through the one mile trip into town from his cabin, Joe found state road 110 blocked by two huge boulders that lay on the road prohibiting passage in either direction. The pair of huge rocks appeared to have been loosened by the previous night's heavy rain and rolled down off the slope that inclined from the edge of the west bound lane of the road. There was insufficient room to drive cautiously around the boulders on either side. The steep angle of the bank made it impossible to skirt right around the boulders. Circling around by the east bound lane was prevented by the abrupt fall off of the land beyond the pavement downward to the bed of the Miwok river. Conscious that he had little time before the citizens of Craterville were expecting their only source of staples and non-perishable food to open, Joe backed up a short distance where he could park off the road and started his walk into Craterville.

Once he opened the store, Joe found that his only insoluble problem was answering to the satisfaction of his questioners inquiries about Carey's condition and when she would return to run the store. Of course, some of this interest was motivated by the absence for more than a week of fresh vegetables, meat and poultry, those features of the normal diet that would be missing unless they made the long drive to Santa Clara until Carey returned. However, Joe could sense that Carey was a respected and well-liked member of the community whose physical difficulty prompted the majority of inquiries about her. His questioners were uniformly unsatisfied by the paucity of the information he could give about Carey's condition and the time table for her return. Joe found that the lack of information about one of their favorite townspeople seemed to produce more apparent annoyance with him than the absence of items they had hoped to purchase.

Joe was completely worn out by the time he closed the store at 6:00 that evening. He did a bit of straightening up so that Mrs. Tejada would be only mildly shocked when she opened the store on Monday at noon. He slid the day's cash and credit card bills through the narrow slot in the side of the heavy safe to which only Carey had the combination. Weary and satisfied, he locked the store for the day. He had only taken a few steps from the door when he remembered that his car was not here in the parking lot, but a little more than a half-mile away, beyond the rocks that had obstructed his drive into town that morning. He decided to return to the store and get a flashlight to help him make his way safely through the fading daylight. He did not expect to encounter vehicles between Craterville and his car unless the obstructing rocks had been cleared, but a misstep could put him in the same place or predicament as Carey.

He quickly re-entered the store, got himself a new flashlight and supplied it with batteries. He realized then that having emergency lighting at the cabin was a precaution that he had overlooked. He also decided to take a second flashlight and batteries to keep in his car. He smiled and made a mental note to tell Carey that she had made money even after closing. He stood in the parking lot considering whether to treat himself to dinner at the Niner before he walked to his car when he heard a short toot from a vehicle horn. Joe turned and saw Evan Iverson's truck roll up beside him and stop.

Iverson lowered the driver's side window and grinned. "Hey, store keeper, how did it go?" he asked.

As Joe mulled his response, Jimmy Chinn got out of the passenger side of the truck and greeted Joe. "Did everything go O.K., Mr. Bell?" Jimmy asked.

Joe nodded at the tall, broad-shouldered boy, who seemed always to be smiling, and said, "Everything went fine, Jimmy. I planned to get the key back to you after I got some dinner so you could open the store after school on Monday. Let me just give it to you now."

Jimmy pocketed the offered key as Joe asked, "How did your meet go?"

The boy looked embarrassed and was still searching for his response when Iverson said, "You're looking at the district pentathlon champ, Joe."

"That's great, Jimmy, congratulations," Joe said and offered his hand.

Jimmy responded to Joe's grip shyly. However, the strength in his young hand was evident. Joe was not entirely sure what combination of running and field events constituted the pentathlon; however, he did not find it hard to envision Jimmy's excelling athletically. The boy's chest was broad and muscular and his torso tapered to a small, trim waist. Joe had previously noted the litheness of Jimmy's movements as the boy worked in the store. Having been told by Carey that Jimmy was an outstanding student, Joe was doubly impressed by his athletic success. "Good job, Jimmy," Joe said. "Carey will be pleased."

"Would you tell her I'm sorry I haven't gotten over to see her, Mr. Bell?" Jimmy asked.

"Sure, Jimmy, I'm sure she understands," Joe assured the boy. "And I know she appreciates your taking care of the store," Joe added.

As Jimmy turned to get back in the truck, Evan said, "Why don't you hop in too, Joe? I'll take you to your car after I drop Jimmy off."

"You know about my little problem in getting here this morning?" Joe asked.

"Oh, yeh," Evan answered, "word about the rock slide was all around town by mid-morning Slides are not all that rare after a heavy rain."

Joe accepted Iverson's offer and squeezed in beside Jimmy for the short ride to the boy's home. In a few minutes, Evan stopped and Joe stepped out of the truck to let Jimmy get by. He returned to his seat and watched the boy wave as he entered his house. "He's a good kid," Joe said.

"And a very talented one," Iverson said. "He's got it all. The grades, a hard-working, competitive attitude and a world of athletic ability. No one even came close to him in total points today."

"How'd you get to the meet? I thought you had a septic tank emergency today," Joe asked.

"I got it finished early. Got there about half way through the meet. Just in time to see Jimmy bury the competition in the 1500 meters." Joe was surprised at Evan's enthusiasm. Evan saw his expression and explained, "I'm a long time track and field junkie."

"I knew there had to be something besides your work that interested you, or you wouldn't have that unique scheduling and billing system of yours," Joe smiled.

"Preserving some free time for other interests is just one of the reasons for my system, Joe. It's too long a story to get into." On that note they rode silently out of town toward Joe's car. As they approached the spot where the rock slide had blocked the road that morning, they saw that it had been removed. Evan drove the short additional distance to Joe's car.

Evan killed his engine and Joe got out of the truck. As Joe thanked Evan for the ride and started for his car, Evan said, "It's the least I can do for the man who saved Craterville from starvation." Joe gestured a good natured rejection of the exaggeration. Iverson re-started his engine and pulled away a few feet and then stopped. "Hey Joe," he called. "You'd be able to fill in for Jimmy next Saturday if Carey can't make other arrangements, won't you? You know the kid will skip the competition rather than let Carey down, don't you?"

"I haven't committed to anything for next Saturday yet." Joe said honestly.

"It's the final step to the state meet, Joe," Iverson explained earnestly. Somehow that statement was supposed to be both self-explanatory and totally convincing.

"If necessary, I will," Joe decided. Iverson gestured his thanks and drove off.

The next day, Joe described to Carey both his first day as a grocery man and his dialogue with Evan about the coming Saturday. "So you see," Joe concluded as he finished his report, "the immediate threat of famine in Craterville has been lifted. However, there may be evolving the largest concentration of freezer section vegetarians west of the Rockies."

Carey, her left leg now encased from the ankle to the hip in a very solid looking cast, frowned fretfully. "Maybe I could make a few phone calls and get some fresh vegetables and a small number of packaged portions of the more popular cuts of beef and chicken delivered during one day in the week. Probably most of them would sell before they're past usability. I need to think about re-stocking the shelves of prepared foods anyway. Jimmy and Mrs. T. can help me to do that by phone. About next Saturday, Joe," Carey sighed and scrunched her face apologetically, "I hope I can impose on you one more time. Even if the doctors let me go home in a few days, they're insisting that I stay off the leg completely for at least a week at home. I'm going to be stuck in my apartment over the store for some time."

Joe gestured a dismissal of her concern. "Don't worry about it. I'll handle things Saturday and in whatever other way I can help. Think of all the new skills I'm developing. What a fall back career I'll have if I never get published."

"Hey," Carey chided. "Don't even joke about not getting published. Your first novel is going to be the first hard back book ever stocked and sold in the history of the Craterville grocery," Carey insisted emphatically. Joe could not remember ever having heard anything that pleased him more, though his only response was a smile.

9

ON MONDAY, AFTER A morning more memorable for its industry than its output, Joe realized that he had not used his day as a store keeper to do his own grocery shopping, He decided to get to the store while Mrs. Tejada had it open from noon to 2:00 p.m. As Joe entered town at the east end of Sutter Street, he passed a sheriff's department patrol car and an officer standing beside a car at the curb talking to its driver. He assumed a ticket was being issued; however, when he got to the grocery store parking lot, Joe concluded that something out of the ordinary was happening. There was another sheriff's patrol car parked near the store entrance, and two officers stood at the door of the store. As Joe neared the door, one of the officers touched the brim his hat in an informal salute and offered a courteous greeting. He smiled and asked, "Would you take the time to give us some information, sir?"

Joe nodded his willingness. The unusual amiability of the officer prevented Joe's feeling the uneasiness that he invariably felt in his few experiences with a lawman. "Do you live around here, sir?" asked the deputy sheriff, a designation Joe noted from the man's shoulder patch.

"About a mile east of town," Joe answered tersely.

"Did you try to drive into town on Saturday and find the road blocked?" the deputy asked.

"I did," Joe nodded. "I walked into town from the slide."

"The slide?" queried the other deputy, who had been silent until then.

"I assume that's the blockage the deputy asked about," Joe explained to his new questioner. "The rocks that slid on to the road after the rain on Friday night."

There was an interlude of silence before Joe's initial questioner said, "We think it's likely that the blockage didn't result from the rain, sir. That's why we're making inquiries. Did you see or hear anything out of the ordinary Friday night? Maybe a truck with a winch working after dark? Something like that?"

Joe nodded. "No. I didn't see or hear anything out of the ordinary. Of course, my cabin's a bit more than a half mile from where the rocks were in the road. And it sits back from the road as well."

"How about when you stopped at the blockage," asked the more aggressive of the pair, "there wasn't a vehicle or person positioning the stones to be sure the road was blocked?"

Joe shook his head, "No. Besides," Joe added, "obviously I'd have asked what was going on if there'd been anyone at the blockage."

"Unless you thought blocking the road was a good idea," the edgy deputy pointedly countered.

Joe bristled and was about to object to the officer's implication when his amiable colleague injected, "Hold on, Hank, I don't think that we're prepared to inquire yet about anyone supporting those tactics."

"Tactics?" Joe frowned with honest puzzlement, "What tactics?

"Well, sir," began the friendly deputy, "there was another road blockage that turned up this morning about six miles east of town.

It seems clear that it wasn't a slide. Someone's perpetrating some very serious and dangerous vandalism."

"You mean deliberately pushing boulders on to the road?" Joe asked.

"Pushing's not quite the word for it," said the bristly deputy. "Just starting them rolling so that they'll end up on the road."

The deputy's description made the task of moving and placing the sizable rocks, if, in fact, anyone had done such a thing, seem unconvincingly simple and easy to Joe. "I realize you're the experienced investigators, but--" Joe began and then stopped when he realized the officers might not take kindly to his expressed doubts.

"But?" asked the easy deputy.

"Well," Joe began in response to the invitation, "From the size of the two rocks I saw, it would take both great effort and skill to get one of those things moving, even on a downward slope. Secondly, one would have to be lucky about where each rock stopped if the intent were to block the road. Finally, there's practically no traffic on route 110 east of town because it's a dead end. Why would a person do all that work to pull a prank when there's no one to annoy except for about a dozen people, like me, who live pretty far east of town?"

"The prank was not meant to annoy residents but was meant to annoy Sierra Logging," asserted the aggressive deputy.

"I guess you haven't noticed that there haven't been any logging trucks going through town this morning," offered the amiable deputy.

Joe was slow to respond, He was trying to absorb the possibility that a group was trying to sabotage the logging activity. Finally, Joe did say, "I hadn't noticed."

"Of course," smiled the amiable deputy, "these blockages can't have much effect, It doesn't take a front loader long to push the rocks, even ones the size used in the blockages, off the road down toward the river bed. Hardly seems worth the effort to put the rocks in the road."

"Especially to risk jail time on a felony conviction," the aggressive deputy added ominously.

The implied warning made Joe smile. He wondered if the hostile deputy was going to try to stop the vandalism by threatening everyone in town. Joe pulled open the door to the store and smiled the smile of the amused innocent at the deputies. "It's surprising what people will sometimes do just to make a point," he said as he proceeded to his shopping.

Sometime later, Joe emerged from the store laden with his purchases to find the deputies still at their task with another arriving shopper. He put his groceries in the trunk of his car and was about to drive off when he succumbed to his curiosity that had been building ever since the deputies had questioned him.

What would long time locals have to say about the interrogations being conducted in their normally tranquil town? No doubt the full variety of opinions could be heard at the Niner diner. He decided he needed a coffee break at the Niner before he returned to his cabin.

Joe found that he needed not inquire what local folks made of the interrogations being conducted by the sheriff's department. He no sooner sat down and ordered coffee and a plain donut than he was addressed by a man he knew only as a nodding acquaintance. "Joe," the man began, using a familiarity that Joe had not previously been accorded. "Did the sheriff's deputies question you?"

Joe struggled for a moment to try to come up with the man's name before he gave up, counting on a grin to convey that he was returning the man's familiarity. "Yes. I got the full good-cop, bad-cop routine."

"Probably not, Joe," nodded another man among the four sitting with his initial questioner. "That Deputy Skinner, the shorter, husky one; he's just a grouchy son-of-a-bitch all the time. Hell, he'd put cuffs on his own mother if he stopped her for speeding. Ain't that right?" he asked, swiveling his head to take in all the men seated with him. Having received the anticipated affirmative nods, he asked Joe, "You think there's anything to their theory that someone's rolling rocks onto the road?"

"Seems an unlikely feat to me," Joe said.

The initial speaker nodded toward one of his colleagues, "Hal thinks it could be done, don't you Hal?"

A rugged looking man with a weathered face looked at his table mate who had addressed him and said, "Hell, everyone here knows it could be done, if you find the right spot with a couple of well-placed rocks that are pretty round. Must be dozens of men in town have the kind of pneumatic jack that would start a good sized round rock rolling down if you did a little digging before hand." Offering Joe a crooked grin, Hal continued. "Course none of these lazy bastards sitting here could do it, Joe. But there are men in town who know how to put their backs into a little physical labor."

"Hell," injected a new participant in the conversation, "I wouldn't do all that work when all it takes for a front loader to push the damn things off the road is about ten minutes."

"That's the mystery, isn't it?" said Joe's original questioner. "What reason would anyone have for going to all that trouble for so little result? What do you think, Joe?"

"Maybe someone thinks that if they keep it up, the company will eventually route the trucks around town, even though the blockages haven't been much more than an annoyance," Joe offered.

One man who had not spoken before said, "That's a dead issue. The company will never give up going through town. If someone's rolling boulders, they'll run out of rocks in good position to be used before the company gives in."

"There's another possibility," said the man who had started the conversation. "Maybe the boulder rollers don't expect to accomplish anything. Maybe they just want to do some payback for Carey Siebold's broken leg."

"But Carey doesn't hold the logging truck responsible for her injury," Joe pointed out.

"She wouldn't," said the man called Hal, "even if she believed the truck was responsible. She's a fighter, but she's got the damnest rules about limits on conflict." There was nodding all around, showing the respect in which Craterville's leading activist was held.

Joe downed the last bit of his donut and followed it with the last swallow of his coffee and got up to go. "So I guess we'll have to leave the solution to the mystery of the rolling boulders in the hands of the deputies."

"You're not going to hold your breath till that happens, are you Joe?" someone asked.

"No," Joe responded with a wry grin. "Truth is, I wouldn't bet that it will be solved before my year's lease on the cabin runs out." Amid the general laughter that occurred, Joe waved to the five men as he exited the diner.

In fact, word was not abroad three days later that the deputies had arrested anyone for the vandalism, nor did the investigation seem to have great urgency because there had not been any new blockages on route 110 between the logging site and Craterville. However, the dawn of the fourth day rose on not one but two blockages on state road 110. For the first time, one pair of well-placed rocks was on the road west of town. This obstruction took a bit longer to clear than the two on past mornings, since the one east of town was reported by the logging company immediately after the start of their work day. The county's highway maintenance garage and the sheriff's department sent all available equipment and investigative personnel to the site of the first report, since it was assumed that a single vandalism had occurred as in the previous instances. To the frustration of the authorities, the obstruction west of town, which was reported an hour after the first one, produced more notice and comment. That section of the road, which ran from Craterville to Santa Clara, was more heavily traveled than the dead end portion to the east of town, which was traveled by few people other than the logging trucks.

Annoyance with the disruption of easy travel was no longer limited to the Sierra Logging and Lumber company. However, amusement at the situation was more widespread as well. The anonymous boulder roller or rollers were admired for ingenuity and illusiveness. That the perpetrator's activities were not doing any significant damage to the logging company beyond brief irritation deprived the firm of sympathy. Many were amused by this tweaking of the nose of an entity with money and power that normally got things its own way. While the anonymous pranksters would have drawn substantial ire if people had been injured or seriously inconvenienced, there had been neither injuries or lengthy stoppages.

This latest harassment contained a feature which for the first time left the vandal's purpose beyond question. Each of the rocks had the message *stop the trucks* painted on it in fluorescent white paint. The perpetrators had apparently belatedly realized that the rocks would not show up sufficiently in the dark if a motorist were unwary or speeding. The fluorescent paint greatly diminished this possibility. This concern for the safety of motorists besides the message asserting the goal desired encouraged people to enjoy the campaign of harassment of the company. Most conversations about the event centered on wondering how long the activities of the sole or group of gadflies would continue before they were apprehended or the opportunities for mischief were used up.

10

ON THE DAY OF the double blockage, Joe began his daily evening visit with Carey with an account of the latest vandalism and the generally amused reaction to it in Craterville. Carey stared into space thoughtfully for several minutes after Joe finished his story. Joe assumed she was mulling over the situation and was being careful to phrase her reaction. He was surprised when Carey refrained from reacting to the news and asked him if he would go down to the shop in the hospital lobby and get her a copy of the Santa Clara daily paper, The Sierra Intelligencer. When he returned, Carey was just completing a phone call. She did not immediately peruse the paper Joe placed beside her but rather began a series of questions about topics of discussion in Craterville other than the vandalism. Joe found it obvious that she was avoiding the subject of the campaign of harassment of Sierra Logging. Since his circle of acquaintance in Craterville was much less extensive than Carey's, he could not answer many of her questions about specific people and their activities.

When Joe apologized for his lack of information, Carey smiled and said, "Not a problem, Joe. I'm just killing time." She was silent for a few minutes again before she sighed and asked, "Joe, I need another favor."

Following his response that he would do whatever he could, Carey said, "I hate to impose on you again, but if I can get them to let me go home tomorrow, would you come and drive me back to my apartment?"

"If you can handle the trip in the confines of my car with that leg, of course I'll take you. The front passenger seat reclines. Maybe we could use some folded up blankets to support your leg."

Carey nodded. "That'll work just fine."

"What's your hurry, Carey?" Joe asked with some concern. "We can handle things for you at the store. Why take a chance on leaving the care you have here too soon?"

The negative shake of Carey's head was emphatic. "I need to get back to town as soon as possible."

"To do what? You can't get around at all. Who's going to look after you?"

"I'll work something out. Please don't make me try to explain anything. Believe me, the less said the better." Carey said with unemotional finality.

Joe shrugged his shoulders. "If they tell you that you can leave, give me a call and I'll be here an hour later to pick you up."

It was clear to Joe that Carey was no longer in the mood for small talk that avoided the subject that apparently was intruding on her attention. He wrote down the phone numbers for his cabin and his cell phone for her, wished her well and concluded his visit.

A few minutes after noon the next day, Carey called Joe to tell him that she was being discharged shortly. Satisfying himself that he had enough blankets to take along without stripping the one from his bed, he was soon on his way to Santa Clara. An hour later, Carey was suitably positioned in his car to make the trip back to Craterville, notwithstanding the doctor's repeated concerns that Carey was being unwise to leave hospital care. During the trip, when Joe echoed the doctor's concerns, Carey assured him that she would be fine. She reported that Mrs. Tejada had found someone both reliable and trustworthy who could spend days with Carey until she was on her feet.

As though to underscore Mrs. Tejada's appraisal, Mrs. Hernandez was waiting for them at the door of the stairway up to Carey's apartment on the second floor of the grocery store building. Unfortunately she had unsettling news to relate. An as yet undiagnosed problem was disrupting the town's water system. Carey's building, like every other structure in town, was at the moment without water. The mayor had announced that arrangements had been made for tank trucks to arrive with water that residents could carry from the trucks back to their homes until the town's water system was restored. However these arrangements were not expected to be in operation for some hours yet, possibly not until tomorrow morning at the latest. Mrs. Hernandez reported that the entire stock of bottled water in the store had been sold fifteen minutes after Mrs. Tejada had opened at noon.

Joe turned to Carey, whom he as yet had not lifted from his car, and said, "Looks to me like you have two options, I can take you back to the hospital, or I can put you up at my place, which has its own well."

Carey sighed and thought for a moment before asking, "Would you mind terribly if I stayed with you?"

"If you're willing to risk my cooking, I'd be delighted to have you," Joe offered sincerely.

Carey thanked Mrs. Hernandez for her readiness and said she would be in touch about future arrangements when the matter of the water supply was cleared up. After the short drive to his cabin, Joe carried his visitor to the most comfortable chair he had, arranged her leg most carefully on a low stool and placed her wheel chair within reach. As he explained that he would need some time to prepare his bedroom for her use, Carey was profuse in repeating her promise to be as little trouble as possible. Joe's assurances were emphatic that he did not feel imposed on by whatever actions he would have to take on her behalf. On reflection, he realized that he meant what he said even more so than he would have anticipated. In fact it was apparent in a few hours that they would manage quite well, partly because the few doorways and the short hallway were wide enough for Carey to get through in her wheel chair. Also, the tables and countertops were the right height for her use while seated in her wheel chair.

Joe was a bit concerned that Carey's spirit of independence in getting in and out of her wheel chair to sit in a regular chair were a flirtation with disaster, but Carey was insistent that she must be as self-sufficient as possible for someone with the full length of one leg in a cast. Carey was so emphatic that Joe's normal routine was to be preserved as much as possible that he spent some time writing the evening of her arrival although it was not his usual time to write and the unsettled circumstances did not yet favor the task of writing.

The next morning, as Joe was finishing several hours of struggling to re-awaken the flow of his writing, Carey wheeled herself out of the bedroom to which she had insisted on sequestering herself while he wrote. She moved her cell phone from her lap to the table that stood beside what she and Joe now referred to as *her* chair. Carey reported that Mrs. Tejada had informed her that water was flowing once again through the water system of the town of Craterville. Unfortunately it was not because the town's wells were pumping into the town's reservoir water tank as normal. The town's water tank was being filled by tank trucks provided at no cost by Sierra Logging and Lumber. The mayor announced that he had arranged with the logging company that the trucks would be used free of charge to the town to fill the town's reservoir tank until the water table was restored to the level at which the town's pumps could operate.

Carey had also been told that the mystery of the lowered water table had been solved. In the process of the highway department's removing the boulders that had blocked the highway, several rock slides had been started by the boulders as they rolled down the ravine to the Miwok River. The flow of the stream had not actually been stopped, but it was theorized that the slides had somehow affected the underground water table. Conviction that the slides were the cause of the water problem was not universal; however, no one had a more plausible theory.

Carey asked if Joe could tolerate her intrusion for one more day. Meanwhile, Mrs. Hernandez would help Mrs. Tejada re-stock the store and make some re-arrangements of Carey's apartment that Carey thought would make it more manageable for her return. Carey pleaded that she would have to trouble him no longer than another day. Joe insisted that Carey had been no trouble. He told her that she might be underestimating the amount of time her two helpers would need to complete their tasks. He suggested that she stay with him several more days. Carey expressed her reluctance to stay the longer period. Joe suggested she think about his offer while he went for a walk.

About a half-hour later, Joe set foot on the porch as he returned from his brief walk and heard Carey apparently on the phone. She sounded more strident than what Joe had come to recognize as her usual conversational style.

"No, no," he heard her say, "What else could it be?" She was silent for a few moments. "You just promise to stop. Promise. I mean it." There was more silence. "O.K. then," Joe heard before the return to silence indicated the conversation had ended.

Joe entered the house and Carey turned in her wheel chair at the sound of his entry. Her smile surprised him "Hi," she said and dropped her cell phone into her lap.

"Everything O.K.?" Joe asked.

"Just a stubborn supplier," Carey explained. Offering another smile, she asked, "How about some lunch? My turn to fix it."

Joe laughed, "How could I explain letting a woman in a wheel chair make me lunch when she doesn't even know where anything is?"

"That's a point," Carey conceded. "Can I at least be in charge of the drinks?"

"As long as you don't skimp," Joe said as he went into the kitchen. Joe made them a pair of passable sandwiches with his diminishing supply of sliced ham and cheese. To Carey's sandwich, he added mayonnaise, which he now knew that she favored over mustard. Meanwhile, Carey wheeled about the kitchen pouring two glasses of wine and starting a pot of coffee. They almost collided once near the end of their labors, and Carey followed her chuckle at the near collision by saying, "You'll be relieved when I'm out of your hair tomorrow morning."

It was not mere courtesy when Joe responded that he would miss the company when she was gone. The afternoon and evening were spent by the pair in a mood punctuated by remarks by each that would have made one think that Carey was going on a long voyage rather than all of a half-mile to her apartment in town. The next morning, the feel of Carey's body in his arms as Joe carried her up the stairs to her apartment increased his disappointment that Carey's visit with him was ending.

11

JOE DID NOT SEE Carey or hear from her for three days after he carried her up the stairs of her apartment and left her in the solicitous care of Mrs. Hernandez. However, at noon on the fourth day after Carey had left, he answered his phone and heard Carey say, "I hope you've been good and put in your time at writing this morning."

Joe responded jovially, "My conscience is clear in that respect although perhaps not so guilt free on other matters."

Carey made a tongue-clicking sound of disapproval and said, "Well, sometime you must confess to me the full record of the many things you have a guilty conscience about, but today I am calling with another shameless request for a favor."

"You know that I can deny you nothing," Joe responded with an air of exaggerated melodrama.

"I won't tell you what any sensible woman would say to such a statement because I'm am forced to beg."

"Don't be absurd," Joe said seriously. "What do you need?"

"The doctor is willing to x-ray me tomorrow to see if my knee's healed enough to permit him to remove part of my cast. I thought that I had a ride to the hospital, but it now appears I don't, so I wonder if I may prevail on you again to take me to Santa Clara?"

Joe quickly gave his assent and their travel arrangements were quickly concluded.

Joe arrived at the entry to Carey's apartment at 7:15 the next morning as agreed, which would give them ample time to reach the hospital in Santa Clara for Carey's scheduled 9:00 a.m. x-ray. As Joe approached the doorway to the stairs up to Carey's apartment, he was addressed by a young woman who had been standing nearby. Noting the several books and the notebook that she was clutching to her chest, Joe concluded that the girl was one of the high school aged youngsters who waited on the Sutter street side of the grocery store for the bus that took high school aged students to school in Santa Clara.

Joe stopped at the doorway. The creamy-complexioned, pretty blonde approached somewhat shyly and asked, "Are you going up to see Carey Siebold?"

Joe nodded and said that he was, The girl lowered her pale blue eyes toward the ground, and asked, "Would you ask her if I could speak to her, please?"

"I'll ask her," Joe said. "What's your name?"

"Honor Purefoy," the girl responded. "She knows me." The girl shrugged her shoulders. "She knows all the kids, really. In bad weather she opens the store early and lets us wait for the bus inside."

Joe said, "She has to leave for a doctor's appointment soon. I'll tell her you're here, and she'll decide if she can take the time to talk to you." Joe opened the door and climbed the stairs. He paused on the landing outside the apartment door. In response to his knock, he heard Carey tell him that the door was not locked. Joe entered and, after a brief greeting, told Carey about the girl who wanted to see her.

Carey thought for only a few moments before asking Joe to tell the girl to come up. Joe went down the stairs to invite the girl up and trailed her into the apartment, where Carey smiled at her and said, "Good morning, Honor."

"Good morning," the girl responded and lapsed into silence.

Joe was puzzled at her behavior, since she had seemed so anxious to speak with Carey. Carey apparently concluded that she was reluctant to speak in Joe's presence. Carey asked Joe if he would get her blue jacket from the closet down the hall. Joe concluded that he was not to return too soon. With the jacket in hand, he did not return until Carey called to him.

Carey handed him a slip of paper, which she explained had the combination to the safe in the store written on it. She asked Joe to open the safe in the store downstairs and bring her the metal box which he would find on the top shelf inside.

When Joe returned with the metal container which was about the size of a shoe box, he placed it in Carey's lap. Carey had a key in her hand to unlock it. Since Joe stood nearby and Carey made no attempt to shield the contents from view, he saw that the box contained two smaller boxes. One was a dark blue flat box slightly larger than the case for an expensive pen and pencil set. Joe saw a design of five interlocking rings imprinted on the top of the velvet-covered box. It took a few moments before Joe recognized the design as the symbol of the Olympic games.

The other container within the metal lock box was a carton which, from the illustration on the cartoon contained individual packets of hard candy each packet in a variety of flavors. Joe's cursory glance at the lettering on the cartoon, which said **The Choice Is Always Yours** indicated no brand familiar to him. Carey opened the cartoon of candy boxes and handed one small packet of the candy to Honor Purefoy. The girl quickly stuffed the candy into her coat pocket, muttered a brief thanks and was gone out of the apartment in an instant.

Carey quickly returned the cartoon of candy to the metal box and re-locked it. Joe asked, "Want me to put it back in the safe?"

"If you would, please, Joe," Carey responded. "I'll be ready to go by the time you get back."

Joe handed Carey the paper on which she had written the combination. "I won't need this to lock up," he said. "And don't worry. I didn't write it down, and I don't have that good a memory."

"I trust you," Carey smiled. "That's why I haven't had to kill you," she added with exaggerated gravity,

Joe smiled broadly as he sighed and turned to exit the apartment, "Wow, I had a narrow escape." He could not remember another woman with whom he had ever enjoyed the sort of absurd and pleasant conversations that he had with Carey.

Upon Joe's return from his brief task, he performed the more enjoyable one of carrying Carey down to his car and beginning their journey to the hospital in Santa Clara.

12

DURING THE DRIVE TO Santa Clara, Joe had a difficult time restraining his curiosity about why Carey kept a box of candy inside a locked box inside a very sturdy safe that was impenetrable except by the most violent or sophisticated means. If the other item in the lock box contained, as it was reasonable to assume, an Olympic medal, he could understand keeping it secure, but securing the candy similarly seemed strange. However, Carey was understandably focused on her x-ray and the possibility that an improvement in the condition of her injured leg might make possible the removal of part of her cast. That would permit her to use crutches and begin the process of returning to a normal life.

Joe had spent a restless hour and a half in one of the hospital waiting areas leafing through some well-pawed and ancient fishing magazines and regretting his having forgotten to bring a book to read. His mood changed instantly when he saw Carey and a nurse coming down the hall. He needed not ask if Carey's leg had improved. She was receiving instruction in the use of crutches as the nurse hovered near her while Carey proceeded with one cautious step at a time. As her injured leg swung forward with each planting of her crutches, Joe saw that her cast now began below her knee and curled around her still-encased ankle. She moved by putting her weight on her uninjured leg and the crutches. Carey looked so happy that Joe could not help but share the feeling.

"It appears your knee, at least. is improved," Joe said as Carey came to a stop before him.

"It's coming along. It will be fine if I regularly do the exercises they gave me. The ankle shouldn't take much longer." Carey thanked the nurse who had been assisting her and assured her that she was now in capable hands. Turning toward the elevators with a deft placement of her crutches, Carey said, "Come on. I'm buying lunch to celebrate."

Later, as they were driving home, Joe decided that Carey's good mood would permit him to risk an inquiry into the mystery of the candy she kept under lock and key. "Carey," he began warily, "I'm curious about something that's so clearly none of my business that I hope you'll not take offense at my asking."

"What's that?' she responded and gave no sign of guardedness.

"Why do you have what looks like a cartoon with boxes of ordinary candy inside a locked metal box inside a very secure safe?"

Carey kept her eyes on the road and gestured dismissively. "Oh, that. It's silly, really. There is among the candies in each box a particular flavor of lime candy that is the most irresistible item in the entire store to young shop lifters for some reason. So I just decided to get temptation out of their way."

Joe found the explanation so unconvincing that he remained silent. Obviously, merely placing the candy under the counter or within the locked case in the store that held the cigarettes would be sufficient security to remove the lure of stealing lime-flavored hard candy. Furthermore, he could not fathom the desire to purchase lime-flavored candy being so intense that a youngster would go to the trouble that the young lady had this morning. If he did not have the absolute confidence in Carey's probity that he did, he would have concluded that the little boxes of multi-colored paper contained an illicit drug rather than candy.

His silence apparently convinced Carey of the dubious nature of her explanation. She sighed and said, "I know what you'd thinking, I'm over-reacting to a very minor shop-lifting problem. It's not the loss of a few cents that matters. I hate to catch a kid in the act. Word of what they've done is all over town in a few hours. And other kids are merciless in their barbs to anyone I've caught."

"Your looking out for the kids is commendable," Joe said, now convinced he should abandon the topic since Carey's elaborate explanation hid more than it revealed. "I guess I never realized the irresistibility of lime-flavored hard candy."

"Just one of the many mysterious things that only grocers get to know," Carey said, looking at him rather than straight ahead for the first time since Joe had introduced the topic.

They rode silently for another fifteen minutes before Joe initiated conversation again. "Were you in the Olympics?"

"Ah, you saw the other item in the lock box as well," Carey concluded. There was a noticeable pause before she answered, "I was never in the Olympics, but someone who was gave me a medal."

"Gave you a medal he or she had won in competition?"

"Yes," Carey answered. "It's a long story with enough dreariness to it that it's not worth repeating."

"Sounds pretty intriguing to me," Joe pressed.

"Well, it isn't," Carey said with an emphasis that signaled that the topic was closed. Their conversation for the rest of the trip was exclusively about the clear and bright weather and the spectacular surroundings through which they were driving. Their mutual earnestness on these overly familiar topics underscored their desire to be amiable rather than risk disagreement by being candid.

When they reached the stairs to Carey's apartment, Joe offered to carry her up the stairs rather than have her make the arduous climb using crutches for the first time. He was not surprised when she refused, insisting that she had to begin managing this barrier to her returning to a normal life. Joe saw her point, but, in the light of the day's experiences with Carey, he wondered if anything about her was truly normal. Between her activism and her evasiveness, she seemed like anything but that uninteresting thing that usually passed for normal. He followed along behind her step-by-step as she labored her way up to her apartment.

Joe declined Carey's offer to come in for refreshment; however, he emphasized that if she needed help with either logistics or the store, she should not hesitate to call. Her thanks were genuine. She added that she had intruded on his writing routine far too long and too often and would try to avoid further diversion of his time and energy. Joe did not say so but felt that he did not regret a moment spent with her or on her behalf.

13

JOE WAS SO ABSORBED in his work for the next few days that the rest of humanity in general and Carey in particular received no more than an occasional moment of his attention. During brief losses of concentration, he felt guilty for abandoning his injured friend. Of course, Carey did have the assistance of Mrs. Hernandez, he knew. Besides, he reasoned that if Carey needed his assistance, she knew how to reach him.

And reach him she did, one day beyond a week from when they had made their trip to Santa Clara. He went to Carey's apartment that evening as she had asked. Joe found her seated in a comfortable upholstered chair with her injured leg propped up on a hassock before her with her crutches close at hand. Evan Iverson sat on the couch which was placed at right angles to Carey's chair. Evan got up and greeted him with a hand outstretched. Joe returned the greeting as he gripped Evan's offered hand.

"Thanks for coming, Joe," Carey said and motioned him to join Everson on the couch. Carey looked tense. The atmosphere seemed anything but relaxed. Joe thought that he might be interrupting a quarrel; yet Evan did not look as uneasy as Carey. "There's fresh coffee if you want some," Carey said.

Joe declined refreshment and looked from Carey to Evan and back again, wondering who would tell him why he had been asked to come. Evan turned to face Joe and inquired, "You've got business contacts in San Francisco, don't you Joe?"

"A few," Joe said tentatively. "I worked in one of the bigger advertising agencies in town."

As Iverson was collecting his thoughts to continue, Carey injected, "I tried to explain to Evan that he can't expect that you'd know anyone in corporate management or ownership other than a few people in the companies you did ads for, Joe."

Iverson raised his hands palm outward as though to push away Carey's statement. "But he might know people who would know someone or some place to ask, is all I'm saying," Iverson countered.

Joe thought he might forestall the renewal of a dispute. "Sounds like I'm hearing the late stages of a discussion. Maybe someone ought to fill me in from the beginning."

"Yes, why don't you do that, Evan?" Carey said with some tartness in her voice.

"Of course," Evan said agreeably, "I should have explained why I thought you might be able to help me. Sorry." His look at Carey showed that his apology was solely for Joe. "You know, of course, about the town's water problem." After Joe nodded, Evan continued. "The authorities have said--and most people have agreed--" he paused and threw an unfriendly glance at Carey, "that the cause of the town's wells failing is the boulders that have ended up in the river from clearing the highway blockages. That doesn't make any sense. How could a minor surface effect screw up a major subterranean water table? It can't." Everson paused perhaps to emphasize the incontestability of his conclusion.

Joe saw that Carey made no attempt to hide her skepticism. Everson answered her look with a confident assertion. "I have found the real reason that the town's wells have gone dry."

"That's good news," Joe said, "especially if the problem's correctable."

"Oh, it's correctable all right," Iverson asserted, "if we can just identify the person who's draining off the entire usable supply."

"I don't understand?"

"You ever notice a brand of bottled water called Sierra Springs, Joe?" Evan asked.

"I can't say that I have, but I don't drink bottled water, so I really haven't looked at labels," Joe answered.

"Well, it's around," Evan said. "In fact, there's some in the store downstairs, which is not surprising, since it's bottled right here in Craterville."

Joe looked at Carey. She shrugged her shoulders and said, "News to me. I carry several brands. The only time I ever glanced at the label, it said that it's bottled by a company in Santa Clara."

"Be that as it may," Iverson said, "it's actually bottled right outside of town in a building on a property owned by something called the Santa Clara Mountain Water Company. There's a well on the property which is busily pumping out water to be bottled. So much water, in fact, that the water table had been lowered to the extent that the city wells have gone dry."

"If that's the case," Carey said testily, "why hasn't their well gone dry too?"

"As I told you several times before Joe got here," grumbled Evan impatiently, "they probably have a deeper well into the same water table."

Joe looked at Carey, whom he regarded as one of the most rational people he had ever known. "You don't believe this?"

"I might consider the possibility if it weren't so important to Evan that it be the explanation of the water problem rather than the one that's been stated to the town council," Carey said with a sigh.

Joe was puzzled. His head turned from one to the other of his companions several times. After a lengthy silence, Carey said to Iverson, "Why don't you tell Joe? Why don't you tell him why you're so interested in water bottling being the reason for the water problem?"

Iverson's annoyance with Carey was unmistakable. He pressed his lips together as though he had to keep words from escaping. Carey offered a challenge, "I'm sure that Joe can be trusted with your little secret." She seemed to be daring Iverson to reveal something to Joe. "You can trust him," Carey repeated to Iverson with emphasis. "Besides, if you want him to help you, don't you think that he deserves to know why you're interested in his help?"

Evan looked at Carey rather than Joe and said, "I'm the one who rolled the boulders onto the highway. That one," Iverson said, rotating his forearm to point a thumb in Carey's direction, "is upset because I retaliated for their trying to run her down."

"Which they didn't do, as I've explained repeatedly to that one," Carey said and duplicated the thumb pointing gesture that Iverson had used.

Joe sensed that this was not the first time that the pair were adversaries. There was likely some history between them that he would be unwise to suggest was influencing their views on the current subject. Besides, he had no desire to complicate his life by becoming a counselor. Taking as much of a risk as he dared, Joe said to Carey, "Carey, I'm convinced by your explanation of how you were injured. However, whether your injury was accidental or deliberate, Evan's explanation of the water problem seems to me more rational than the one that's been given by the authorities."

"All right," Carey conceded, "but you'd better think carefully about what Evan wants you to do and why he wants you to do it before you involve yourself."

Joe nodded his agreement with her caution. "You know how carefully I'm guarding my time, let alone avoiding involvements," he said, more for Evan's consumption than Carey's. "I'll just listen to what he has in mind and then decide if I'm going to do anything. It most likely is something I couldn't do even if I wanted to." Joe turned to Evan and prepared to listen critically.

Evan fixed a serious expression on his face and said, "I want to find out who owns the Santa Clara Mountain Water Company. I suspect it is someone here in Craterville. He or she needs to be called to account publicly for what has happened to the Craterville water system for his or her personal profit."

Joe smiled at the ease with which he could avoid involvement and not refuse Evan assistance. "The company's most likely incorporated. Ownership would be a matter of public record in that case."

Evan shook his head negatively. "I already tried that. Santa Clara Mountain Water is owned by Ariba Enterprises, which is headquartered in Mexico. I can't find out anything about that outfit."

Joe asked, "I take it ownership couldn't be identified by simply going to the plant here in Craterville or the office in Santa Clara and asking?"

Evan shrugged and answered, "If it could, I'd know who the owner is already."

Joe was genuinely puzzled. "Sounds to me that you've tried what could be explored. What do you expect me to do?"

"If the company has its advertising designed and promoted out of San Francisco, maybe the advertising agency has dealt with the owner and could tell you his name."

"There're are at least three big 'if's' in that approach, Evan," Joe said. "*If* the company uses a San Francisco agency, and *if* I can find out which one, and *if* they deal with the owner rather than the manager of the office in Santa Clara, I might--or might not—be able to find out who he is."

Evan nodded affirmatively. "I understand that it's a long shot. I'd just like to have you give it a try."

"And this request to waste your time, Joe," Carey began, emphasizing each word with a jab of her thumb toward Evan, "is coming from a guy who arranges his work to give him the maximum amount of free time, even if someone has to wait for a repair." Carey gave Evan a sideways glance of irritation to cap her point.

"That's not so for critical repairs," Evan countered. "She knows I handle emergencies immediately. Furthermore, I always give people a list of other repair people if they don't want to wait for me to do a non-essential project."

"Which is why people call him Eventually Iverson, Joe, in case you may not yet have heard," Carey said a bit contemptuously.

Joe thought it wise to avoid comment on Carey's statements. He sat quietly for a while. His companions waited expectantly, no doubt with contrary desires and expectations. Finally, Joe said, "I'll make a few phone calls. No traveling to the city; no time-consuming digging; just a few phone calls."

Evan smiled. "O.K., that's all I could ask," he said. With one side-to-side shake of her head, Carey signaled that she believed Joe had made a mistake. Her mood during the remaining few minutes of Joe's stay underscored her doubts about the wisdom of what Joe had agreed to do. When Joe took his leave, Evan Iverson remained. That fact, as much as anything else about the peculiar evening, was puzzling to Joe.

14

JOE KNEW IT WAS too much to expect that a call to Hobson, Curtis and Company, the advertising agency where he had worked, would produce the name that Evan Iverson wanted, but it was the only place he could think of to start. In choosing whom to contact, his decided that his former love interest there would be an unwise choice. Considering her mood at their parting, Joe was convinced that a call to her would be brief, unproductive and a bit unpleasant. He chose to call Dom De Lassandro, who had also been and still probably was a copy writer with H and C, as employees called the agency.

Aware of the vagaries of employment in the advertising business, Joe would not have been astonished to be told De Lassandro was no longer there although it was barely four months since Joe had left. Joe took it as a good omen that Dom not only was there but also seemed pleased to be hearing from Joe.

After a full reporting to one another on the current state of their lives, Joe turned to the reason for his call. Dom was quickly able to tell Joe that H and C did not have Santa Clara Mountain Water as a client. The men chatted amiably for a few more minutes, agreed to get together at some unspecified time in the future and ended their call. Joe pondered what his next step should be. He doubted that he would get any response if he were simply to phone every agency in town and ask for the names of their clients. Whether they served the water company or not, they were sure to brush off an inquiry from a stranger. Either they wouldn't want to be bothered or would conclude that it was not in their interest to get an imagined competitor in touch with their client.

Joe called Dom again and pleaded earnestly for assistance. Joe asked if Dom could think of anyone who might know who did the water company's advertising, assuming it was done in the city. Dom's suggestion was obvious enough that Joe was embarrassed that he had not thought of it himself. His former colleague suggested calling one of the business writers for the San Francisco paper. Dom convinced Joe that the most likely source was the journalist who wrote a local business news column. This column contained a compilation of brief items announcing who had been hired or promoted, what companies had re-organized or merged and similar matters of interest within the local business community.

Annoyed with himself for the first time that he did not subscribe to the San Francisco paper, Joe drove into Craterville to get a copy of that day's edition. Fortunately, the business news column carried a byline. Mercifully, the business writer proved easy to reach. She informed Joe that the ads for Santa Clara Mountain Water were done by a small San Francisco agency called Horizon Advertising. She then asked why Joe wanted to know. With a facility that he was sure would produce guilt on reflection, Joe told the journalist that he was a former copy writer who was thinking of getting back into the business. He said that he was working up copy for a hypothetical campaign for the water company, which he would use as an example of his work if he could get an interview. When the woman wished him luck, Joe further tested the bounty of fate by asking if she knew the name of anyone at Horizon that he could call. She did not, but said that Horizon was a small operation.

Its staffing was not so specialized and layered that he would have trouble reaching the person in charge of hiring by calling their one listed number.

Joe wondered what plausible reason he could give for calling Horizon and asking for the name of the person at Santa Clara Mountain Springs that the Horizon dealt with about the water company's advertising work. No doubt such a question would make Horizon think that he was trying to steal their client. He needed a story that would seem to make it to their benefit to give the information. He left his chair and began a troubled pacing of his living area. The need to concoct stories to get information that was really none of his business troubled his conscience. On the other hand, it was for a good cause, or at least what he thought was a good cause. That reasoning did not help his tranquility much. He then decided not to look on this task from a moral perspective. How about treating it as an exercise in developing his imagination for writing?

This rationalization not only relieved his conscience but opened his mind. The feeling was like having come up with the next plausible episode in a story by freeing himself from the story line that had brought him to a dead end. Freed from his scruples, Joe soon came up with a ploy which had him punching in the numbers of the Horizon Agency phone number.

In response to the greeting at the agency, Joe spoke as pleasantly and authoritatively as his uncertainties would allow. "Hello, I need to speak to the person who handles your accounts receivable about our bill, please." He hoped that a matter related to money coming into the agency would give him an entry. He was not wrong. He was transferred to a Mr. Soderberg.

Joe's past experience in business told him that maintaining a confident air and using the listener's name would enhance his plausibility. "Mr. Soderberg," he began, "I am with the accounting firm of Haverill Accounting in Santa Clara. I am conducting an internal audit of Santa Clara Mountain Water Company. I merely want to confirm that the last bill you sent has been paid."

Soderberg asked Joe to wait. In a brief time, he responded that the last bill had been paid.

"You're sure the check cleared?" Joe asked.

"It did," Soderberg responded. "Why? Is there a problem?"

"Not if the check cleared," Joe said tersely and paused, hoping the silence might entice Soderberg to continue the call.

"We have valued Mountain Water as a client," Soderberg said, concern beginning to creep into his voice. "We hope nothing's started to go wrong."

"No cause for concern at your end, I assure you," Joe said, pausing again and hoping to be considered mysterious. "I take it that your interactions with the personnel of the company have been satisfactory."

"Oh, yes. Mr. Harrison is great to work with. He's receptive to our ideas, but is candid at saying what he likes or doesn't. He has proposed some good ideas of his own."

Joe suddenly realized that he had not found out from Evan the name of the manager of the water company office in Santa Clara. He had no idea if Harrison was the owner or merely an employee. To keep the dialogue going so he might eventually get more relevant information, he asked, "So no problems, I take it?"

Soderberg was slow in responding. "Not really."

"If there is anything, Mr. Soderberg, it would be helpful for my client to know," Joe said, striving for earnestness.

"There was an abrasive session that one time that he had that woman with him," Soderberg said with reluctance.

"Who was that?"

"We never did get a name, but Harrison obviously deferred to her."

Joe permitted himself a restrained chuckle before asking, "She was a bit aggressive?"

"Let's say she doesn't need assertiveness training," Soderberg said, matching Joe's restraint. "She has a temper to match that red hair."

Joe could not see any way that he could ask if the aggressive woman was the owner of the company, or he would not seem to know who his employer was. "Well, If financial matters are in good shape and the working relationship has been primarily positive, I think that you've given me everything I need, Mr. Soderberg. Thank you."

"You're welcome, sir. Give my regards to Mr. Harrison."

Joe said he would and ended the conversation hastily, especially since Soderberg had not asked for his name and Joe wanted to avoid inventing one.

Joe considered it unlikely that Harrison owned the water company since he had deferred to the unnamed assertive lady who had accompanied him to the ad agency on one occasion; however the likelihood that Harrison was an employee should be confirmed. Because Evan Iverson had dealt with the Mountain Springs Santa Clara office, he would most likely know whether the Mr. Harrison that Soderberg mentioned was an employee or a possible owner of the company. Joe doubted that he could reach Evan during the normal work day, so he called the handyman's number expecting to leave a message requesting a return call. To his surprise, Iverson answered the phone. Joe confessed his surprise and Iverson said that he was not working for the rest of the week.

Mindful of Iverson's work mode in which reaching a week's income goal limited the work week, Joe said that he was glad things were going well for Evan. Evan sounded slightly impatient in asking the purpose of Joe's call. Suppressing a tart reminder to the handyman that Evan had asked for his help, Joe briefly summarized his efforts and concluded, "Do you know if Harrison is the office manager in Santa Clara or might he be the owner of the company?"

"He is the man I talked to there," Iverson said, "He's just an employee."

"Well, the red-haired lady might be the owner, then, since Harrison was deferential toward her," Joe concluded.

"Unless she's just Harrison's opinionated wife," Iverson reasoned.

"True, but we've got nothing else to go on. Does it sound too bizarre to you that we try to find out if Harrison's wife is a redhead?" Joe asked. "We could at least eliminate that possibility."

"Let's save that for a last resort," Iverson suggested. "Let's try something else first. Let's assume that the owner is a Craterville resident, since the bottling plant is here. Why don't we consider all the red-haired women in Craterville and decide if there is a promising candidate among them."

"Do you know who all the redheads in Craterville are, Evan?" Joe asked with some skepticism.

"I don't," Iverson admitted. "I'll admit that on the spur of the moment I can't think of one redhead I do know who is a good guess to be a closet business owner, but we both know someone who can probably identify the possibilities for us."

Joe could supply the name of that person himself. "You are thinking of one Ms. Carey Siebold."

"Yes," Iverson replied. "Why don't we meet at her place tonight at seven after she closes the store?"

"See you there," Joe said and concluded the call.

15

STANDING RATHER CONFIDENTLY ON her crutches, Carey invited the two men into her apartment with a mixture of amusement and wariness. "I'm surprised to see you have fallen into frequently spending time in bad company so soon after moving to Craterville, Joe."

"Ah," Evan said and drew the sound out and accompanied it with a smile. "That's the Carey Siebold that we all love--sweet, fair-minded and never sarcastic."

"Some people could force sarcasm out of a saint," Carey retorted as she made her way back to her usual chair and sat down, leaned her crutches against the low table beside her chair. She propped her leg on a hassock and relaxed comfortably, obviously satisfied with her management of her circumstances.

Evan sat on the couch and scoffed, "How would you know what tries the patience of a saint? Not personal experience, I'm sure."

Carey was about to respond when Joe intruded, "I can see there is a longstanding sparring match between you two. I don't want to referee it, and neither one of you would like my psychoanalysis of it."

"Oh, dear," Carey said with an exaggerated sigh, "I hope that convoluted psychoanalyzing isn't your bent as a writer. I'll never be able to stay awake through one of your books."

"I didn't mean for you to simply shift targets," Joe chided Carey.

"Yeh, what's wrong with you, Siebold?" said Iverson, deflecting blame away from himself with playful cynicism.

"Why don't you just tell the lady why we're here?" Joe suggested and seated himself on the couch next to Evan.

Evan sat back comfortably and summarized the scant results of Joe's efforts. He focused on Carey and stated, "We thought that you could speculate on who among the red-headed women in Craterville might be the owner of the Santa Clara Mountain Springs bottled water company."

Carey shook her head in disbelief. "How absurd. You want me to pick a target for you? For you to do what? Harass her about your theory that the bottling has taken the town's water?"

"Harass?" Evan challenged. "Why would it be harassment to ask her to cut back bottling for a couple weeks to see if the water table is restored?"

"What if a rumor starts and makes every woman in town with red hair the object of suspicion when you don't know if the owner even lives in town or that the bottling is the problem?" Carey argued. Joe had to admit that he had not considered such a possibility.

"Don't you think we can be discrete?" Evan responded. Joe was surprised and unnerved by Evan's including him in his investigation, but he did not say so.

"Do I even have to answer that?' Carey asked and could not restrain her look of amusement.

"I think that you've just afraid that I'll turn out to be right," Evan accused.

"Really?"

"Yeh. And that I could be right about the so-called accident as well," Evan pressed on.

Carey looked combative. "If I thought you could look into something quietly without confrontation--" she paused without finishing her thought.

Evan sensed an opening. "It might not be wise of you to accuse anyone else of being confrontational. Besides, you don't have any reason to believe that Joe couldn't be quite subtle and discrete in dealing with anyone you suggested."

"Me?" Joe gasped with alarm.

"You're the logical person, Joe," Evan said with complete aplomb, as though he had stated something that was clear from the outset of this exploration.

Joe was quick to disagree. "I don't see anything of the sort."

"I've already talked to someone at the plant and at the office in Santa Clara," Evan explained. "Obviously the owner has been informed. She would be on her guard the moment I approached her," Evan reasoned. "Whoever it is wouldn't admit ownership. It will have to be inferred from the answers to some innocent-seeming questions," Evan explained.

"Still," Joe began, genuinely at sea, "I haven't the faintest idea how to approach anyone on something like this."

"No one would," Evan said with perfect patience. "You'd just have to feel your way."

Carey was smiling broadly. "Yes, Joe, just listen to Mr. Subtlety there."

"You're not funny," Evan grumbled.

"Maybe not," Carey said, enjoying Evan's displeasure. "But I'll tell you this. I'd never give you a name for you to approach yourself."

"But you would to Joe?" Evan asked hopefully.

"Possibly."

"See, Joe, you've got to do it," Even said with satisfaction.

"She just said 'possibly,'" Joe said, feeling trapped.

"Well, Carey, are you going to tell us a name, or are you so afraid that I'll be right that you won't say?"

"I'll tell Joe alone," Carey asserted, "if he's the one who would look into it rather than you."

"I don't want to do this," Joe said with anguish. "I never wanted to get involved in any of this."

"Joe, you can't back out now," Evan said.

"I don't have to back out; I never got in."

Carey was obviously enjoying herself. Evan stood abruptly. "I think I should go. You and Carey talk, Joe."

Joe looked at Carey. She said, "Stay and have a cup of coffee, Joe. We can talk about the sad state of Evan's sanity, if nothing else."

Against his better judgment, which was shouting that he should flee, Joe remained seated. Carey grabbed her crutches and pulled herself to her feet and started toward the kitchen, presumably to make the coffee she had offered. Joe could not believe that he was not following Evan down the steps.

In a few minutes, Carey said from the kitchen, "I can't bring the coffee out there, Joe. Will you come and get it?" Joe hurried to assist and brought the tray with the coffee pot and two cups back to the living room, where he set the tray on the table in front of the couch. Carey returned to her chair. Joe served her and himself cups of the steaming black liquid and returned to his seat.

"Sorry I can't be more of a host, Joe," Carey said and sipped her coffee.

"Not a problem," Joe assured her. "The coffee's great."

They lapsed into silence, giving the coffee much more attention than necessary for consumption. With apparent reluctance, Carey asked, "Joe, I wonder if you'd be willing to tell Evan that I've given you a name and that you'd approached the woman and discovered no connection to the water bottling company?"

"You mean even though you haven't given me a name at all?" he asked. Carey nodded affirmatively. Joe was surprised that Carey was asking him to lie. "Carey, I'm not afraid to tell Evan that I don't want to pursue the matter."

"It never crossed my mind that you might be afraid to refuse," Carey hastened to say earnestly. "You don't know Evan. He'll never let go of his idea until the avenues of pursuing it have been exhausted. We have to stop this before he begins approaching every woman with red hair that he runs into."

"Do you and I have to resort to such an elaborate deception? Why not just say that our discussion didn't produce any plausible name to be checked out?"

"That would launch Even into a campaign of his own that would turn this town up side down."

"You think that there's no chance that he could be on to something?" Joe asked.

Carey sighed resignedly. "I'll admit that bottling water, if it's been increased lately, could be affecting the wells. That's something that can be explored through normal channels. We do have a government in town, after all. They could follow up once the possibility is called to their attention. There's no need for this undercover stuff. No matter who owns the company, the bottling plant can be approached directly by the town government and asked if they've increased operations lately."

"And you think they'll admit it if they've caused a problem and would be willing to cut back their bottling?" Joe asked. Carey nodded affirmatively but looked uncertain enough that Joe said, "You don't look very sure."

Carey could not hide her frustration. "*If* the water's bottled here, and *if* the manager's a woman, I can't see that confronting her would accomplish anything either," Carey said.

Carey's phrasing suggested to Joe that Carey was thinking of a specific person rather that an abstraction. Joe studied Carey's face carefully. "You actually have someone in mind, don't you?"

Carey's face showed signs of a struggle. "Maybe."

"Ah, evasiveness," Joe sighed a feigned sound of disappointment. "I've never had this experience before with Craterville's official public conscience."

"That's enough of that," Carey responded testily.

"Do you have a name in mind?"

"Of course," Carey confessed uneasily, "and so would Eventually Iverson if women existed for him concretely enough to see us with features and everything."

"Aren't you going to tell me?'

Carey looked at Joe pointedly. "And what sort of mess would you make with the information if I did tell you?"

"Actually," Joe began, "I don't even know if I want the information. You know how desperately I want to avoid involvement. However, I admit that if I knew the name you have in mind, I might not be able to resist trying to find out if she's the owner of the water bottling company. If she is, I'd pass the information on to Evan so he could make his accusations."

Carey jabbed a finger in Joe's direction. "Which might create a local controversy that would tear this town apart."

"Maybe not. Maybe it would be the beginning of getting things back to normal," Joe reasoned. Then, although he could hardly believe he was saying it when he did, he said, "Why don't you just give me the name and I'll decide whether or not to follow up? If I do follow up, I'll decide to what extent I can discretely work on it. If I don't know anything conclusive, I'll refuse to tell Evan a who or what."

Carey looked at Joe steadily for a while. "I wish that I knew you better."

"I wish you did too. However, I'd like to think that would take years," Joe said.

There was another silence of considerable length. "Marsha Sulliband." Carey breathed the name almost despairingly. "She might be the redhead in question," Carey added with obvious reluctance.

"The mayor's wife?"

"Yes. She's a very intense business woman. She runs the family real estate agency. The extent of her business activity is beyond that of any other woman in town," Carey said.

"Why wouldn't Evan have thought of such an obvious possibility?" Joe mused.

"She's only occasionally red-haired," Carey explained. "Her hair's naturally brown, but she occasionally tints it. Quite a nice auburn, actually. Evan may never have seen her sporting the color."

It occurred to Joe that common sense made Mrs. Sulliband a poor prospect. "If she were the owner of the bottling company, the mayor would surely have considered that there would be a connection between the volume of water bottled and the effect on the town's water supply."

"Good point," Carey agreed with enthusiasm. "You see why she's not an obvious possibility. Besides, there aren't any other women I can think of as possibilities. The likelihood is that the plant's not locally owned. A better way to dispose of Evan's theory is a direct approach to the council. The council might explore the possibility of bottling affecting the water supply and perhaps become local heroes over the outcome."

Joe felt a sense of relief. The secretive activity that Evan had in mind seemed totally unnecessary. "I'm comfortable to tell Evan that it's wiser that the council be approached directly about the possibility of checking into the bottling as a cause of the town's water problem."

"Would you feel obliged to mention Marsha Sulliband as a possible owner?" Carey asked apprehensively.

"I think that would make Evan unnecessarily accusatory in approaching the council and the mayor, don't you?" Joe said.

"It would be a minor miracle that he wouldn't be accusatory if he thought there were any chance that the mayor's wife is connected to the water bottling," Carey chuckled.

Joe stood and prepared to take his leave. "I'm glad this discussion has turned to using an approach which is not fraught with controversy."

"Or one that will tempt you to distraction from your work," Carey added. They said their good nights both satisfied with how their evening had turned out.

16

AS A RESULT OF his evening with Evan and Carey, Joe decided to wait several days before speaking to Evan. He would at that time say that he had found no definitive connection to the water bottling company and the woman whom Carey had identified for him. No doubt Evan would pressure him to reveal her identity to him. However he was sure that he could resist that pressure by insisting that it was unnecessary for Evan to know that name because the only appropriate action was to urge the town council to explore the matter of bottling possibly affecting the water supply.

For two days, he devoted myself to his work and the daily routine that he had come to find so satisfying since coming to his mountain retreat. Joe was confident that Evan Iverson would find his position not only defensible but wise. Unfortunately, Joe's common sense failed him after a couple of days. An innocent way that he could approach Marsha Sulliband for a conversation occurred to him. Perhaps a dialogue on a real estate matter could stray into a revelation of the other information that was of meaningful concern to Evan and the community at large. Joe's overmatched common sense kept reminding him that the road to hell truly was paved with good intentions, but finally his weaking good sense failed him, and he entered the swamp of involvement.

He called the Sulliband Realty Company and made an appointment to meet with Mrs. Sulliband to discuss buying a building lot. The receptionist tried to schedule him with one of the firm's associates; however, he insisted that he was only interested in meeting with Mrs. Sulliband. Having secured that appointment for the next day, he proceeded to do a little preparation that would permit him to give the an air of plausibility to his meeting with the realtor.

He drove through Craterville to the town's western outskirts. He wanted to examine the water bottling building and its surroundings, which had previously escaped his notice until Evan Iverson told him of its existence. The briefest examination of the site showed that it would suit to set up the ploy he would use in his meeting with Mrs. Sulliband at the real estate office. The windowless, metal building sat back from the highway on the western edge of a broad, slightly rolling, wooded meadow that extended several hundred yards eastward from the plant itself. Among good-sized ponderosa pines and sugar pines bordering the meadow, one would have a very attractive and practical home site if one could acquire an acre or more along the paved road. Even though Joe's real purpose in having a conversation with the realtor was to elicit a revelation regarding the ownership of the bottling business, an inquiry about a home sight at the location in question was a reasonable subject for inquiry by a person who was currently renting nearby.

The next day, when Joe entered Mrs. Sulliband's office for his appointment, he got the immediate impression that this was not a woman to be dealt with recklessly. As she rose and came around her desk to greet him, she stood several inches taller than Joe's five feet nine inches by virtue of her spike-heeled shoes. She looked to Joe to be in her late thirties. Her tailored, navy suit outlined her curvaceous body attractively but not too snuggly. Her figure had retained the enticements of youth and was now accompanied other attractions that fortunate mature women grow into—an engaging, confident smile, a smooth, clear complexion, and an unstudied seductiveness of movement. In short, she had allure that escapes most fresh, young beauties.

Joe noted that her hair color, which Carey had told him varied from time to time, was not red at the moment. It was likely that a well-chosen tint would result in her hair being an auburn shade that would cause Mrs. Sulliband to be described as a redhead. Joe noted that her shoulder-length hair was currently what he would call chestnut colored. He also concluded that her milky complexion would go well with the auburn color. She a very attractive woman. Joe cautioned himself not to become distracted from his covert purpose.

Marsha Sulliband was quite businesslike in shaking Joe's hand and offering him a seat before she returned to her chair behind her desk. Before beginning his response to her routine question of how she could assist him, "I'm considering settling in Craterville permanently, Mrs. Sulliband," Joe explained.

"Call me Marsha, please," Mrs. Sulliband smiled at Joe. "You look familiar. Are you living in town now?'

"Close by. I'm renting a place about half a mile east of town," Joe said.

"I thought I'd seen you around, but I don't know your name."

"It's Joe Bell."

"Welcome to Craterville, Mr. Bell. The local supply of young handsome strangers is not extensive," Marsha Sulliband said turning up the wattage on her smile considerably.

Joe responded cautiously. "Thank you. I've been here several months. It suits me. That's why I'm thinking about staying."

"You're single?" she asked and continued after Joe's affirmative nod. "We have very few listings available in town, but there are a couple choice small places if you're interested in something toward the upper end of the market."

"I could handle a substantial down payment; however, I'm not in a position to handle a big monthly mortgage," Joe said truthfully.

"What sort of work do you do, Mr. Bell—or may I call you Joe?" Marsha Sulliband asked with an air that indicated no male had ever turned her down on such a request.

"I prefer Joe. I'm an aspiring writer," Joe said.

Joe had not thought that the woman could project more attractiveness than she had already, but with a widening of her eyes and a broadening smile, she said, "How exciting. We really must find something for you. The town could use an addition to its intellectual population."

Joe felt embarrassed. "Well, I'm not sure that my presence does anything of the sort. I'm really just trying to get started."

"And Craterville's a wonderful place to do it. I can't wait to show you our listings," she said.

"Actually," Joe began warily. "I have been considering something other than an existing dwelling. I was wondering if a home site could be acquired at reasonable cost so that I could proceed to build on it as my finances permitted."

Mrs. Sulliband smiled sympathetically at Joe's idea. "This area is a much prized location for residential and recreational development. Open land is not only scarce and consequently not modestly priced."

"That's surprising," Joe responded. "There seems to be so much open space around. There's a beautiful open area just west of town that looks like a gorgeous place to build."

Marsha Sulliband nodded knowingly. "That sounds like Broadbent Meadow. It is a pretty spot; however, it's entirely owned by one of our local businesses. I'm afraid it isn't up for sale."

"Not even an acre or so bordering on the highway at the eastern most edge of the meadow?" Joe asked.

The handsome woman studied Joe intently with a little smile on her face. "I hadn't thought of that. Her hazel eyes narrowed as her face took on a thoughtful expression. She settled into a deal-maker's expression and said, "Perhaps the possibility of acquiring a home site ought to be discussed at the business in question. Did you notice the building at the far western end of the meadow, back from the highway?"

"I think I know the one you mean," Joe said disingenuously, since he knew exactly the building being referred to.

"There is a dirt lane that winds back toward it at the western end of the meadow where the land begins to slope up into the mountains. If you meet me at that building at five-thirty today, we can see if the owner is willing to consider selling a piece of the property."

Joe was not sure whether he should feel successful at making a step closer to finding out what he and Evan Iverson wanted to know or if he should feel frightened that he was taking one more step deeper into a quicksand of involvement. However, he said that he would be at the building that she had specified at five-thirty. As she warmly escorted him from her office. Marsha Sulliband told him that it might turn out to be an interesting session. Joe was not so sure.

He was even more unsure when he parked in front of the door to the building, which stated its function on a small sign next to the only entrance. It read simply: Sierra Springs Bottled Water. There was only one other car, a late model Cadillac, parked nearby. He noted as he walked toward the door that no sound came from within the building. Operations within the building, whatever they were, seemed to be over for the day. Joe wondered if he had misunderstood Marsha Sulliband's directions about the time for their meeting when the door to the building opened and Mrs. Sulliband greeted him and invited him into the building.

"You're very prompt," she said as she steered him down a short hallway. Arriving at a door lettered with a male name unfamiliar to Joe and labeled *manager*, Mrs. Sullibrand opened the door into a room that served as a reception area to an inner office. The attractive realtor strode through the reception room and into the inner office. Following close behind her, Joe entered a large room with dark cherry wood paneling and wine-colored carpeting. Centered near the wall opposite the door, there was a large desk of a wood of a similar color to the paneling. A large leather couch took up the entire wall facing the desk except for the doorway. A conference-sized table with a couple stacks of files at one side took up the wall to the left of the couch. The general impression Joe garnered was that the office was a bit more lavish than he would have expected for the on-site management of a production operation.

Although the door through which Joe had entered had the title *manager* lettered on its wood exterior, Marsha Sulliband seemed perfectly at home in the room. She walked to an oak wood unit along the wall behind the desk that matched its length and design and had a computer at its center. "There's a map of this property that you should look at on the table, but I thought you might like to have a drink first."

She opened one of the doors in the cabinetry of the unit behind the desk and drew out an ice bucket and two glasses. The tall svelte realtor opened another door and revealed a number of bottles. "I prefer bourbon myself, but, as you can see, there are a variety of choices available."

A drink had been the farthest thing from Joe's mind but for agreeability's sake he said, "Bourbon on the rocks is fine."

Marsha Sujlliband soon had two identical drinks in hand and extended one to Joe. "Here's to a good deal for both of us," she smiled and touched her glass to the one Joe held.

"Sounds good," Joe responded and joined Marsha in each of them sipping their drink.

"The surveyor's map on the table will give you a bird's eye view of the entire property," Marsha said and gripped Joe's elbow to guide him toward the table. "Broadbent meadow is one of the few large flat areas around here. You'll see that this building doesn't break it up in any way."

Slightly distracted by Mrs. Sulliband's nearness and her hand on his arm, Joe went to the table. He saw that his surmise about the property had been correct. Broadbent meadow extended from the western edge of Craterville for several hundred yards along the highway to the beginning of the upward slope which was the western rim of the bowl in which the town lay. He could not locate the dimensions at a glance but a good guess was that the roughly rectangular meadow was half as deep as it was in length along the road. The Miwok River flowed along meadow's back edge rather than dividing it. That made it apparent even to an inexpert person like Joe that the property was a prime site for residential or recreational development. He expressed that sentiment to Marsha Sulliband.

She pressed close to him and put her face near his ear and whispered as if there were some danger of her being overheard. "The owner doesn't feel the time is quite right for developing the site." She paused and moved her lips even closer to his ear as she pressed her soft body against Joe's side. "But, for the right incentive, it might be possible to convince the owner to sell a home site at one edge of the property so that the rest of the tract remains intact.

"Here, for example--" Marsha set down her glass, put one arm around Joe's waist and reached across his body to point to the corner of the meadow along the highway and closest to town. Joe was stirred by the nearness of her. He was conscious of her perfume for the first time. His gaze rose from her finger touching the map up to her smiling red lips. He decided that her lipstick was a good choice with her complexion and hair.

"What sort of incentive to sell are we talking about?" Joe asked, aware that this was the right or wrong question depending on what one wanted to happen next.

"Let's sit down and talk about it," Marsha suggested and steered Joe toward the couch while keeping her arm around his waist. Joe sat down and soon found Marsha seated disturbingly close to him. He wondered if her intentions were what they obviously seemed to be or if this was a sales technique he had not until now encountered. He had to remind himself that his goal in coming had been to uncover the ownership of the water bottling business.

Joe tried for a businesslike demeanor and asked, "I assume that the property is owned by the operators of this plant, which I gather from the sign out front bottles water. If they've not been interested in selling any property up to now, what makes you think they might sell a building lot now?"

Marsha patted Joe's knee and let her hand come to rest on his thigh. "Trust me; I could swing the deal for you if you and I have a meeting of the minds." Joe doubted that Mrs. Sulliband was referring to price, though he felt that wisdom urged that he interpret it as such.

"It is prime land, as you've pointed out," Joe said. "It's probably out of my price range."

"I'm sure something reasonable can be arrived at," Marsha said. "I've got skills for taking care of your needs that you wouldn't believe until you've seen me in action."

Joe was neither a prude nor inexperienced with women but his common sense was telling him that it would be a mistake to respond to Marsha Sulliband's thinly veiled overtures. Besides, maybe they were not overtures at all. While Joe was satisfied that he had a normal amount of masculine appeal, he had never been troubled with beautiful women coming on to him. Furthermore, he had begun this encounter under false pretenses. Even if he were totally amoral, which he never believed he was, he could not avail himself of Marsha Sulliband's abundant charms and then say he was not interested in buying property at all.

"Maybe it would be better if I thought this all over and got back to you," Joe said.

Marsha Sulliband smiled invitingly, "You needn't rush away. Let's forget about business for a minute. How about another drink?"

Joe was still holding the drink he had only sipped once. "No thanks. I think that I'd better go."

"If you're concerned that we might be interrupted, Joe, I can assure you that we won't," Marsha said, rubbing her hand lightly along his thigh.

Joe took Marsha's hand in both of his. "I have to be honest with you. You are a very attractive woman, and I have been keeping to myself for some months now. If I don't leave now, I am liable to do something we will both regret."

"If whatever you're thinking of doing remained our little secret, sweetie, I can assure you my silence can absolutely be counted on." Marsha said with a tone of voice that struck Joe as being more businesslike than seductive.

Searching for the right exit line, Joe pondered his choices. He doubted that Marsha Sulliband was accustomed to rejection. Joe came near not believing that he was himself rejecting a pleasure long absent and so freely offered. However, every consequence of an intimate interlude that he could envision dampened the appeal of the immediate pleasure. Joe steeled himself and said, "Actually, I'm almost certain that I would disappoint you." He rose from the couch quickly, hoping that he had chosen the exit strategy that would be the least annoying to such a palpably desirable and willing woman.

Marsha rose as quickly as he. "I can't believe you're so timid, Joe. Real estate is far from the only thing I could help you with."

"I know I seem very foolish," Joe said. "But I want to stay around Craterville for a while--maybe a long while--and that means avoiding embarrassing notoriety. Secrets always seem to surface.

Someone who's coped with small town life as successfully as you have surely understands that reality better than most people."

Joe watched the coldness that Marsha began to feel register in her face. "I can assure you by my own experience that intimate secrets can be kept even in a small town. However, I've already gone beyond what my pride tells me I should have. You're right about one thing. I understand very well the way small town life works, Joe. So let me make you a promise before you go. If you breathe a word of our meeting today to anyone--and I do mean so much as a single word--you can count on being charged with attempted rape."

Joe gasped. "But I haven't tried anything. Why would you do such a thing?"

"As you pointed out, gossip is a favorite pass time in small towns. I am just as anxious to preserve my reputation as you are yours. If I have to smear you to avoid damage to myself, I will not hesitate to do so. That you didn't do anything won't save you. Do us both a favor and forget you were here today." Marsha curled one side of her mouth for an instant. "Unless, of course, you reconsider that drink and where we'd go from there."

Joe was stunned rather than attracted by Marsha's renewed offer.

"You can count on my silence," he said and turned quickly to exit the room and the building.

On the drive home, Joe alternately felt amusement and frustration. He had refused sex with a very attractive and willing woman, who, though she was perhaps ten years older than his thirty-five years, had physical attributes rare among women Joe's age or younger. Joe could not remember ever having had even a homely woman come on to him so overtly, let alone a beauty. Regardless of Marsha's threat, he might as well remain silent about the encounter. Who would possibly believe him? If his male friends back at the ad agency were told of the incident, they might rush him off for a mental examination after a barrage of negative comments about his masculinity.

When he was not smiling in recollecting the episode, he felt annoyance. He felt that he could reasonably speculate that Marsha Sulliband was the owner. or co-owner with her husband the mayor, of the Santa Clara Mountain Springs Water Company. However, he could not tell Evan Iverson without revealing how he had come to that conclusion. That would immediately lead, he was sure, to his being accused of rape. Even if Iverson were to solemnly promise that he would not divulge his source, the temptation to use the information to restore the town's water system and end the accusation that the road blockages had damaged the water system would be overwhelming. No matter what precautions Evan might take to keep his source secret, Evan's use of the information would inevitably lead to a problem for Joe. For the first time in his life, Joe truly understood why it was said that silence is golden.

17

EVAN IVERSON PACED LIKE a hungry lion back and forth on the porch of Joe's cabin. "Come on Joe, you're being ridiculous." Joe took another sip of his coffee rather than responding. Iverson stopped in front of Joe and said, "You're saying that your follow up on the name that Carey gave you didn't connect the woman in any way with the water bottling company. So why won't you tell me her name."

"What can I tell you beyond what I've said several times already," Joe said with some exasperation. "I'm not saying because I think you'll decide to check out the name yourself. Soon there will be a lot of talk and conflict that will do no one any good, most of all the woman in question."

"I'll be very discrete; I promise," Evan said, pleading emphatically.

Joe grinned wryly. "This from the man who blocks highways solely on the basis of his suspicions that a friend of his might have been intentionally injured. Besides, if you want to make the assertion to the Craterville council that the water bottling is screwing up the town water system, you don't need to know who owns the damn business. Be my guest; talk to the council." Joe hoped that Evan would not follow that last suggestion, but he felt that his appearing not to discourage Evan's pursuing the matter demanded his making the statement.

Evan spread his arms in a gesture of appeal. "Maybe the company can't be stopped legally. Maybe public pressure on the owner is the only thing that will work."

Joe sighed resignedly. "And maybe people won't even believe there's a connection between the bottling and the water problem. Or maybe you're right about their having a legal right to bottle as much water as they want on their own property. Let the council sort it out," Joe urged without much expectation of being listened to.

"So you'd let the company just get away with harming the whole town if they have a legal position about taking all the water they want?" Evan asked accusingly. "Morality, Joe, morality. Ever heard of it?"

"You are in a very poor position to use that argument. Furthermore, I have no desire to set a vigilante action in motion by helping you pursue the matter. Try established channels one time, Evan. You might find you like it," Joe said with as much finality as he could muster in view of his really hoping that Evan would do nothing. Joe understood that he was being self-serving in the argument he was making, but he believed that there was common sense in his position as well. It was frustrating to continue this conversation. Evan showed no sign of ending the dialogue, and Joe was on the verge of losing his temper, a response to which he was prone when he was being disingenuous and his fellow conversationalist was being persistent. No doubt his awareness that he was not telling Evan what he knew was adding to his frustration, but his position was too precarious to even tell Evan why he could not tell him what he wanted to know. The man who had reacted so dramatically to his suspicion that Carey had been intentionally injured might want to take action against the threat to Joe.

"I've got to get back to work, Evan," Joe said and started for the door to his cabin.

Before the door closed, Joe heard Evan say, "You're making a mistake, Joe."

Later, Joe considered that he had not discussed with Carey what had transpired since she had given him Marsha Sulliband's name as a possible owner of the bottling operation, so he called her to see if she was interested in a report.

Carey sounded pleased to hear from him. She said, "Yes, I'm curious about what you've been doing, but more importantly, I'm anxious to have you see the recently improved me. Why don't you come by for dinner at seven tonight?"

Joe readily agreed. He always enjoyed his time with Carey. He suspected that the improvement she had spoken of was the removal of the cast on her leg. He was a little disappointed that she had not asked him to drive her to Santa Clara for that procedure. He would have enjoyed conversing with her during the trip.

He arrived promptly at seven, carrying a bottle of champagne to celebrate the improved Carey Siebold, though he realized it was silly to bring champagne to a woman who had cases of the stuff in her grocery store downstairs from her apartment.

Carey opened the door of her apartment to Joe and stood there smiling broadly. Her tailored slacks made it obvious that the cast on her leg was gone. Though she rested her weight partly on a cane, she stood quite comfortably erect. She took several steps away from the door to demonstrate her mobility, then she pivoted back to face Joe and said, "What do you think? Almost as good as new, right?"

Joe smiled and said, "I'm hardly in a position to disagree when you're holding a potentially lethal weapon."

Carey raised the stout wooden cane to a horizontal position. "I admit, when one is almost done depending on a cane, there is a strong temptation to swing it about for effect." She demonstrated with several swipes of the close-grained, sturdy stick in the air about her.

"I can see that I'd best not try your patience," Joe said with mock apprehensiveness.

Carey waved him toward the living room. "Please come in and I'll do my very best to behave myself."

Joe extended the bottle of champagne. "My contribution to the celebration."

"Thank you," said Carey. "We can use it after we finish the one I have on ice. Would you be good enough to open the chilled one, and I'll get something to whet our appetites for dinner."

Joe went to the ice bucket on the kitchen counter. "I'm glad you're getting along so well."

"It's exhilarating to be able to get around and do everyday things again," Carey said. She removed a tray of bite-sized cheese pieces from the refrigerator, added some crackers to the tray, and took it to the coffee table in the living room.

Joe soon followed her with a flute of champagne in each hand. He handed one to Carey and joined her on the couch. Extending his glass toward her, he offered, "Here's to the progress of your improving agility." Following the toast, they engaged in amiable small talk about Carey's return to operating the grocery store. In about fifteen minutes, the bell of the timer on the stove alerted Carey that her entrée was ready.

"I hope that you not expecting gourmet fare, Joe," Carey said as she went to complete the tasks for bringing the meal to the table, "I favor main stream cookery over the unusual in recipes and presentation."

In fact, Joe found everything from the tossed green salad, to the meat loaf, baked potato and fresh peas an especially savory version of one of his favorite meals, one he had been denied for months because of his limited cooking skills. He could not have been happier when Carey said, 'Nothing but ice cream for dessert, I'm afraid. I am a working girl again, you know." Joe could be sincere in his enthusiasm about both the meal and the dessert to come. The tastiness of the meal was to Joe more impressive since Carey had so recently returned to a full day in the store although she was not fully restored to normal mobility.

When they were re-settled on the couch sipping a coffee flavored liqueur that Carey admitted was a favorite with her, Carey said, "Now, what if anything, have you been able to find out about the possibility that Marsha Sulliband owns the water bottling company?"

Omitting the portion of the episode that had resulted in Marsha Sulliband's threat, Joe said that he was reasonably sure that Marsha Sulliband could be inferred to be the owner of the bottled water company. However, he hastened to add that he had not told Evan Iverson either the name of the person that Carey had identified as a possibility or that she was probably the owner. "I believe that Evan would use that information in a fashion that would make the situation worse rather than better, Carey."

Carey nodded thoughtfully. "You're certainly right about that."

A silence ensued that lasted for several increasingly tense minutes. Joe began with some trepidation, "I respect Evan, Carey. He seems like an admirable person in so many ways. The way he balances work and leisure is a life style that we'd all be wise to emulate. But he seems a bit irrational about this situation."

Carey sighed and said, "I'm afraid so."

Joe discerned that Evan's concerns in the water shortage situation seems rooted in a protectiveness toward Carey that began with the petition over the logging trucks driving through town. "You seem to know him well, Carey. Do you understand why he's so willing to resort to any sort of tactic about this situation?"

"I think so," Carey said.

Another silence ensued. Joe waited for her to elaborate. When she again lapsed into a nervous silence, Joe's curiosity overcame his consciousness that he would be intruding. "Why is he so wrought up about this thing?"

Carey released a long breath and studied Joe a moment before she spoke with obvious reluctance. "You've seen the case containing that Olympic medal that I have."

Joe's brow furrowed at the seemingly total change of subject. He nodded slowly. Carey continued with a look that communicated the revelation of an intimacy. "It's Evan's. A bronze in the decathlon. He won it about twenty years ago. He gave it to me when he asked me to re-new our engagement. He wouldn't take it back even though I said *no* to our engagement."

Once Joe overcame his surprise, he said, "You said 're-new;' then you were engaged once?"

Carey shook her head dismissively to the question. "It's a pointless and not uncommon story. Never mind the details. They're not worth hearing."

"Oh, come on, Carey, you can't give a person a bit of a story like that and not tell the full story. Please."

"Have you ever heard of the Bronze Man of the Decathlon?" Carey asked.

Joe considered himself above the average in his interest in sports, but had to admit that he had not. Carey smiled wryly. "I'm not surprised. Olympic fame is very fleeting when one is not a gold medal winner. Evan took a bronze in the decathlon despite being smaller than the typical size of decathletes, particularly at the international level of competition. He overcame the additional difficulty of sustaining a serious injury in the midst of the decathlon events to take the bronze. For a brief time he got more notoriety than third place winners usually get."

Joe was intrigued. "I had no idea. Evan's still a very fit man but he can't be over five feet ten inches tall and about one hundred and eighty pounds. What little I now about the events in the decathlon is that they require the strength of a bigger man as well as speed."

"Exactly," Carey confirmed. "It was a surprise in most circles that he made the team although he had been pretty successful in college. He trained fanatically for two years before the competition to select the team. He was willing to sacrifice anything to make the team. He insisted we put us--our relationship--on hold for two years while he devoted every minute to training and competing. I broke our engagement about a year into his training. I had to do it by letter, in fact, because he wasn't available to see me just then."

Joe wondered how serious the relationship between Carey and Evan had been, but he could think of no way of asking without it seeming insulting. He opted for sympathetic vagueness. "It must have been hard," he said.

"You can't believe," Carey responded with similar vagueness. "To tell the truth, if I hadn't loved him so much until the breakup, I probably would have reconciled with him afterward."

Her statement sounded contradictory. Joe's face must have shown that and prompted Carey to elaborate. "A love that intense is like a serious disease to which one is immune if one overcomes it after the first time one's infected," said Carey flatly. Joe was surprised at her matter-of-factness. Her delivery reflected genuine conviction and resignation. He wanted to ask if she had ever felt that intensity again, but he dared not risk going too far.

"Is it coincidence you and Evan ended up in the same small town?" Joe asked.

"Oh, no," Carey answered resignedly. "Ever since I refused to reconcile, he's trailed me to every place that a job or career change has taken me."

Joe was puzzled by Carey's apparent coolness toward such enduring attention. She was one of the warmest people he had ever known. He pondered her twenty years of imperviousness to Evan's effort to win her back. "That kind of devotion has not impressed you?" he asked.

"You can call it devotion," Carey responded tartly. "I call it unhealthy obsession. It's what you might expect from someone who was unintentionally tripped and fell during the fifteen hundred meters at the Olympic games and got up, injured shoulder and all, and won the race. Then, the next day, with his broken left shoulder taped to his side, he won the javelin."

Joe was awed. "And he's shown that kind of determination in pursuing you for twenty years," he marveled.

"He's had absolutely no encouragement from me. People who notice his apparent interest in me sometimes point it out to me, assuming that I just haven't noticed it." Carey sighed her exasperation. "I'm sometimes tempted to tell people I'm a lesbian just to stop people's annoying attempts to point out what they think I haven't noticed." She noted the expression on Joe's face and pointed an emphasizing finger toward him and added, "and I'm not gay, mister face-like-a-question-mark."

"So you've just never fallen in love again?" Joe asked.

"No, I haven't," Carey affirmed. "I wish I had. Maybe my tenacious pursuer would disappear."

Joe smiled. "You don't enjoy having an avenging angel standing by in case someone injures to you?"

"After what's happened since my accident, you need an answer to that?"

"What happens now?" Joe wondered as he thought of several disastrous scenarios that could result from Evan's continued actions in response to the current situation. He shook his head and mused aloud. "He's such an admirable man, Carey. Of course, my main concern is my own peace and security, but Evan needs to be saved from himself as well."

One side of Carey's mouth went up with a bit of a smile she failed to suppress. "He is quite a man, Joe, but it does wear thin in a couple decades of trying to deal with his hovering."

"If we could think of some way to take this situation out of his hands; preempt him so he'd be unable to do anything," Joe mused.

"You might as well think about how to stop a wind storm," Carey said fatalistically.

They sat silently for several minutes. Joe sipped the last of his liqueur. Carey reached for her glass but then straightened up suddenly; her expression brightened. "You're right. The only way to stop Evan from doing anything is to do something ourselves."

"Like what?" Joe asked.

Carey's eyes glinted. "Evan's theory is that an increase in the amount of water bottled has drained the town's wells, right?" Joe nodded and Carey continued. "Maybe the bottling should be publicized as an economic plus for the town. If attention could be drawn to the increased water bottling without that attention asserting any connection to the problem with the town's water supply, the possibility of such a connection probably would occur to a number of people. That would lead to scrutiny of a possible connection without any particular individual having to make an aggressive allegation against the company."

"How could we bring such a situation about?" Joe wondered aloud.

"There's a woman in town who is a news stringer for the Santa Clara paper. She's always looking for story ideas. If it's suggested to her that there is a thriving business in the town that is expanding, she would approach the company about doing a story on them, I'm sure."

"What if the company staff asks her where she got her lead? Isn't she going to identify the person for them?" Joe asked warily.

"She's got an e-mail address to which people are encouraged to offer story ideas, and she promises confidentiality," Carey said with the air of a magician completing a successful trick. "If we doubt her promise of confidentiality, we can send the email for the internet café in Santa Clara and use a fake identity."

Joe could think of neither an objection nor a better plan of action than what Carey suggested. He offered his earnest hope that the plan would work as Carey expected and turned his attention to devoting the rest of the evening to pleasant conversation. His curiosity pushed him to want to know more about the relationship between Carey and Evan Iverson, but he suspected that any inquiry on that subject would bring the evening to an immediate and unpleasant end, and he was enjoying himself too much to have than happen. Joe choose a topic he already knew to be of mutual interest. He asked Carey what she happened to be reading at the moment. That began a spirited dialogue that lasted until Joe realized that he was keeping his hostess up past the point where her fatigue from a full day in the store and the preparation of an elaborate dinner was finally apparent to him. His comments in leaving were not an exaggeration when he said that it had been the most pleasant and interesting evening he had spent since moving to Craterville.

18

MILLIE CARSTAIRS HAD TO inquire of several people before she found anyone who knew the location of the Santa Clara Mountain Springs Water Company bottling plant. Like most of Craterville's residents, if she had heard of the existence of the place, she had forgotten it. She was, of course, familiar with the product, since she had seen it and occasionally bought it from the shelves of the Craterville Grocery. The email message from "public spirited citizen" had informed her that the company was in the midst of a surge of growth and suggested that it was worthy of a story as Craterville's most recent and successful new industry. She didn't often do business stories and never did anonymously suggested stories. She most often wrote of local personalities and events; however, industrial development was so rare and welcome an occurrence in the mountain hamlet of Craterville that she agreed with the anonymous source that the bottling company was worthy of exploration as a story. She was a bit puzzled by her source's insistence on confidentiality. Perhaps it had something to do with the fact that her source sold the product and did not want to be seen as promoting a product from which the person profited. Millie thought that was carrying the desire for anonymity too far, but she could see no harm in following up on the suggestion.

Millie had decided that she would go to the plant without having made an appointment. Experience had taught her that interviews often were more substantial and revealing if people did not have time to anticipate questions and prepare answers that were evasive or slanted toward an interviewee's desired result. She stopped her car before the only door she could see as she approached the large building with a corrugated metal exterior. A small sign beside the door stating the company's name told her she had come to the right place. She got out of her car and studied the building briefly as she stepped toward the door. Obviously the building had been designed for the sake of economy and functionality and nothing else. It looked a bit forbidding. However, pursuit of an interesting story had taken her to a number of unusual locations, and she was not apprehensive.

Millie entered and found herself in a hallway that had several doors on each side that appeared to be the entrances to offices. She had only proceeded a few feet down the hall when a man emerged from one of the offices intent of proceeding down the hall away from her when he spotted her. He stopped and said rather bluntly. "What are you doing here?"

His demeanor was surprised rather than defensive. Obviously visitors were a rarity. The middle-aged man was wearing khaki work clothes and carried a few sheets of paper in his hand. "I'm looking for the plant manager." Millie said.

The man's brow furrowed, as though the inquiry was a rarity for him. "You found him," he said.

"I'm a reporter for the Santa Clara paper. I am interested in doing a story about your company and would like to interview you."

"It's not my company."

"I assumed that," Millie said. "What I meant was that I wanted to talk to a person who could give me some information about the business to put in my story, if I decide to write one, that is. I assumed that the manager is the person who could provide that information."

Millie could see the man's apprehension surfacing. He looked worried rather than belligerent when he asked, "What kind of information? I don't think that the owners would want me answering questions about their business."

"Well, I've been given to understand that your business is growing, for example. I don't see how the owners would object to publicity for a growing business. Some publicity would no doubt help the business grow even faster. Surely the owners would like that."

"It's not my job to guess what the owners might like. The one thing I'm sure of is that they like their privacy."

Millie got out her pad and a pen. "Are they local? I could contact them directly, and you wouldn't have to worry about giving me any information that might upset them."

The man's alarm was obvious. "I'm not going to say where they live or what their names are."

Milllie was puzzled. "I don't understand the concern here. New and expanding businesses are rare in our town. I'd think that the townspeople would be pleased to read about the company and certainly the company should be happy to get the favorable publicity. What's the problem?"

"There's not a problem," the man hastened to say. He clearly did not want to raise any suspicions that the company had something to hide. His reluctance to say anything was raising the possibility in Millie's mind that there was something to hide. She tried not to let it show, but apparently it did. The man came a step closer, trying to be conciliatory.

"Look," he offered, "let me talk to the owners and tell them you want to do a story, and they can tell me if they want me to cooperate."

That was a step in the right direction, Millie thought. She put her notepad and pen away. "I'd appreciate that," she said. What she did not say was that she would talk to local residents among whom there were always some who knew of local situations. These people might suggest why there was such reluctance to accept free and favorable publicity. "Let me give you my number so that you can call me." She fished a business card out of her purse and offered it to the man.

He looked at the little rectangle of paper as though it might be dangerous to actually touch. With apparent reluctance he took the card and shoved it into his pants pocket. Millie had seen many cards pocketed so quickly and never be used to make a call to her. "I know you're very busy and might forget. I'll give you a follow up call in a couple of days as a reminder."

"O.K.," was the terse response.

"Silly me," Millie said, trying to be disarming. "I sometimes miss the obvious. I couldn't find you folks in the phone book. Can you give me your number here?"

"We're not in the book," the man admitted guiltily. No wonder he had agreed so readily to a follow up call, Millie realized, since she wouldn't be able to make one if she had left at this point. She retrieved her notepad from her purse and opened it to a blank page. Extending it and her pen toward the man, she suggested, "Why don't you just jot the number down for me?"

He looked like he was being asked to make an additional payment on his income tax, but he wrote down the number and handed pad and pen back to Millie. Millie smiled her special sweet smile meant to put a potential interviewee on notice that he had not heard the last of her. She thanked her quarry before she turned toward the door and her car.

Inevitably, Millie discussed her visit to the bottling plant with Carey, who was one of her frequent and reliable sources. She asked if Carey shared her puzzlement that the company seemed reluctant to have favorable publicity. Carey responded that such reluctance did seem strange. Professing neither knowledge or opinion about the business, Carey did say that the story did seem worthy of Millie's further exploration.

Millie did not lose interest in the story. When she had still not been called by the bottling plant manager in three days, she was about to make her follow up phone call to the bottling plant when a man called her and announced himself as Jack Hasbro, the manager of the water bottling plant. "I talked to the owners and they said that the timing is not right for a story about the business."

"What's bad about the timing, Mr. Hasbro?" Millie asked. "I would think that your expanding production makes it a good time to do a story."

"That's just the point," said Hasbro. "It slipped my mind to tell you that we cut back our bottling operation several days before you came to the plant. You'll have to forgive me. I'm not used to talking to reporters. Anyhow, I'm telling you now that there's nothing to write about."

To Millie, that there was sudden change in the amount of bottling was as much of a reason for a story as the significant increase had been, but she did not say so. Besides, it was unconvincing that Hasbro could have forgotten to mention such a second significant change in his working situation when she first talked to him. "Why have you decided to cut back?"

"The inventory's not moving as fast as we thought it would," Hasbro said. "Our bottles carry a bottling date and a suggested use by date. We don't want a lot of stale water in stock. Obviously, a story about disappointing sales is not something to publicize, from our point of view."

"Oh, dear, are people going to lose their jobs?" Millie asked.

"No, we just cutting out overtime," Hasbro said. Quickly, he added, "I really got to get back to work, lady."

"Just a couple questions?" Millie coaxed.

"Sorry, I'm needed right now," Hasbro said. Then he added a curt goodbye and hung up.

Millie discussed this latest information with Carey Siebold, who was, it seemed to Millie. uncharacteristically vague and unwilling to speculate about what Millie had been told. When she asked Carey if the story was worth further investigation, Carey was so non-committal that Millie was puzzled rather than either discouraged or encouraged. She thanked Carey for her help with the water bottling story and ended the call after she congratulated her longtime acquaintance on Carey's full recovery from her accident.

The next day, Millie was still debating whether or not to pursue the bottling plant story or find a new subject for her shortly due submission to the paper. However, as was occasionally the case, not one but two interesting stories brought themselves to her. Mayor Cal Sulliband called her to disclose that the water levels in the town's wells were nearly restored to normal levels. In a few days the town's wells would be able to fill and keep full the town's reservoir tanks and make unnecessary further trucking of water to keep re-filling the tanks. Millie was quick to ask what had brought about this happy development. The mayor answered that Councilman Reverend Purefoy believed that it was the hand of God, adding that he had no better explanation and was satisfied to believe the reverend's statement.

The mayor then turned to his second reason for calling. With obvious pride in his voice, Sulliband told Millie that he was about to propose to the town council that the town sponsor an event this summer that was certain to stimulate tourism. Millie was quick to inquire what this particular event would be.

The mayor made a surprising answer. Millie gasped and repeated what Sulliband had said. "A re-enactment of the battle of Craterville?" When she had recovered from her shock, she said, "I've never heard of the battle of Craterville."

"Well, there wasn't actually a full scale battle," the mayor admitted. "As you no doubt know, Craterville was founded as a consequence of a gold strike by some soldiers panning the river hereabouts. During the Civil War, there were both the union and southern factions in town who both organized as militias and almost had a shoot out. It was very dramatic. The situation was all explained to me by a man who has done a lot of these Civil War re-enactments. The issue was whether the north or the south would get the gold being produced in Craterville at the time. Naturally its use to buy munitions and equipment was crucial to both governments. You're no doubt familiar with the monument honoring Captain Horace Broadbent that sits in the circle in the highway on the western edge of town. Captain Broadbent led the union detachment that prevailed and assured that the gold shipments regularly were sent to the union authorities in San Francisco.

"But before the matter was settled there was a period when both the local organized militias threatened hostilities. They trained to march, maneuver and improve their shooting for some time. Then the union sympathizers acquired an edge in fire power, a single cannon bought off a ship in San Francisco. The southerners could not match that power and disbanded."

"So there was no battle," Millie concluded.

"Not in the actual sense," Sulliband admitted. "But a dramatization of what very nearly happened can be a legitimate extension of the historical circumstances. The experienced re-enactor that I spoke with assured me that this bit of Craterville history can be the basis for a very dramatic performance. He has staged many such performances that have been done with the correct uniforms and musketry and all the other details that make for a wonderful spectacle. In addition, he will provide the educational displays that are a unique part of his re-enactments. That will add greatly to the interest of the day. We should be able to draw a very large crowd of visitors to Craterville for the event. It will make for a great weekend of business and give the town the exposure that will keep people coming through the entire summer and fall."

"This re-enactment idea sounds very interesting, if re-enactment is the right term," Millie said. "I will want to do a story after you make your proposal to the town council, Mr. Mayor," she added. "I think that the more immediate news is the restoration of the town's water system. Why don't you give me a quote right now that I can use in my story, and I'll start getting reactions from other folks for the piece." Ten minutes later, Millie was still taking notes as it become obvious that the Mayor would not mind if the citizenry assumed that he had played some significant part in the restoration of the underground water table. She finally interrupted him to say that she had more than enough for a start. Thanking him profusely for his help, she said goodbye so that she could begin planning the whole of the article.

19

CAREY AND JOE SAT on the couch in Carey's apartment and listened nervously as Evan Iverson prowled back and forth in front of the couch and re-stated his argument for the third time. He declared again that the restoration of the Craterville water system should not deter him from publicly asserting that the Santa Clara Mountain Springs Water Company was responsible for the town's water system having failed in the first place.

With less patience than she had spoken with previously, Carey repeated that there was no way he could prove his assertion at this point. "All you would do is create a controversy that could never be resolved."

"Of course, it can be proven," Evan said with impatience that matched Carey's. "The people who run the company simply have to admit that their increase in bottling coincided with the drying up of the town wells."

"Oh, I'm sure they're anxious to admit a cause and effect connection between the two events," Joe said as he grinned mirthlessly.

"It's our job to apply the pressure that will bring forth their admission," Evan argued.

Carey turned to Joe and said, "You noted the use of 'our' in that last statement?" Turning to glare at Evan, Carey said, " I can't speak for Joe, but I'm not interested in being dragged into your insane endeavor."

"Count me out too," Joe added quickly.

Evan stood before them, hands on hips. "You two are going to leave me alone on this?" Carey and Joe nodded in unison. Evan grunted his displeasure. "You know, this would be a lot easier if you told me who owns the bottling company," he said to Joe.

Joe answered with measured articulation. "I told you. I didn't with certainty find out."

"Yeh, but you probably can guess," Evan countered. His stare was accusatory, but received no response. Evan gestured expansively. "O.K. so I'll do it the hard way." He turned toward the door. "The town council meeting starts in half an hour. I don't want to be late."

The pair stared at the door that closed behind Evan. "Are you going to go witness the disaster?" Carey asked Joe.

"Strictly as a spectator," Joe underscored.

Carey sighed and stood. "I don't know how long I'll last, but I'll go with you."

When they entered the council chamber, Joe and Carey found that the council meeting had not drawn a large audience. Joe took that to be a good sign. With the local water crisis past, community interest in the council's doings had returned to normal and drew only the incurable political junkies. Perhaps Evan would have a hard time trying to inflame the small audience. Carey spotted Evan sitting in the center of the front row of the spectator seating area. "I suggest we sit as far away for the detonation as possible," she said and nodded toward the vacant last row of the seating.

In a few minutes, council members began to appear behind the raised, long bench at which they sat during the meeting. Mayor Sulliband was the first to arrive. He smiled affably toward the audience as he proceeded to the center one of the five high-backed leather chairs behind the bench. The other councilors displayed a variety of demeanor as they drifted in singly to take their seats. Reverend Purefoy displayed the same hearty effusiveness which was typical of his conduct in his church activities, chatting and shaking hands with each his fellow councilors as he did with his parishioners after Sunday services. H. Lee Sampson, the school principal, was more reserved than Purefoy but he exuded a similar desire to ingratiate himself. He never seemed to feel secure enough in his professional role that he could forego continuously laboring for acceptability. Homer Jepson, the hardware store owner, deported himself with the quiet confidence of the successfully self-employed, unlike Brian Harrison, the forest ranger, who, of the five council members, looked the most like a man who found it a personal honor to have been elected to the council.

The mayor's four colleagues were soon in their seats and conversing in quiet pairs when Sulliband called them to order with a gentle tap of his gavel. "Members of the council," the mayor began, "I hope you will not object to my deviating this evening from the usual order of business to present a matter requiring prompt attention which I think is worthy of your consideration. We have a guest with us tonight who will speak to this matter. He is on a very tight schedule. I therefore want to introduce out of the usual order of business the subject for which I have asked him to come. He will be able to enlarge on my presentation in a way to help you to understand it fully and decide if it merits your support."

The mayor paused for effect and surveyed the audience as well as his fellow councilors before he continued. "I propose that the council endorse an event to be held on a weekend four to six weekends hence that will bring a large number of tourists to Craterville and give our summer trade a great stimulus for the rest of the summer and fall seasons.

"Specifically, the event would be a re-enactment of the battle of Craterville," the mayor paused and raised his hands palm outward, as though to ward off any immediate reaction. "Before anyone hastens to say that there was no battle of Craterville, let me acknowledge that there was no fire fight in the literal sense. However, most of the town's current residents are familiar with the story of the tension between the union and confederate factions in the town during the Civil War. It will only require a little dramatic license to stage a shooting confrontation that very nearly happened. The presentation will acted out with authentic costumes. equipment, and tactics. The mock battle will show viewers a very entertaining spectacle. It should draw a large crowd. The potential for business revenue is obvious.

"I have asked to tonight's meeting a man who has staged literally hundreds of these re-enactments. Some of these events have required the creative enhancement that we need to make our presentation an attractive spectacle. Equally important, I believe that you will find his knowledge of the history of Civil War times quite impressive. Permit me to introduce him now and he will tell you how he envisions the event and its potential, both for commerce and the educational value which will be an integral part of it."

The mayor looked to his right at the end seat of the first row of the audience gallery. "Mr. Nettleton, would you please stand so that I can introduce you to the council and the townspeople who have joined us tonight."

A tall man who looked to be in his mid-forties stood and turned to face the audience. Joe almost let an audible chuckle escape his lips. One feature of the man's appearance made him identifiable as the Civil War re-enactor even if no further introduction were made. His long, almost gaunt face sported a Van Dyke beard of the kind that was common during the time of the conflict between the states. The broad, pointed mustache and narrow, triangular chin beard emphasized the length of his face. He held his spare, wide-shouldered frame erect. Joe had no trouble imagining him in the uniform of a Civil War officer.

"Our guest," the mayor began, "is Mr. Robert B. Nettleton. For over a decade, Mr. Nettleton has operated a non-profit business in staging Civil War re-enactments. I have asked him to describe the specifics of the re-enactment and other features of the event he will plan and stage if we engage him to do so."

Nettleton nodded to the mayor and did a quarter turn so that he faced both the council and audience in profile. "Thank you, Mayor Sulliband. Members of the council and citizens of Craterville, I am pleased to be here this evening." Focusing on the audience, Nettleton smiled, "As the mayor said, I have been doing Civil War re-enactments for a long time. I have been the organizer as well as a participant in re-enactments on most of the major battlefields of the War between the States in the Eastern United States where an accurate recreation of the past is presented. In addition, from my research I have identified certain historical situations that had the potential to become violent because the stakes were high.

The tension between the confederate and union gold miners in Craterville in 1863 was one such situation. We all know that a huge shift in the balance of power occurred before any event happened to trigger an actual battle. History shows us many instances where just that kind of triggering incident did occur and a battle broke out. The Craterville situation of 1863 is an historical situation that can be projected hypothetically in a way that will be both dramatic and educational. The presentation would start with the actual historical event and then heighten the drama with a plausible extension of what might likely have happened. It will make an exciting afternoon for a multitude of present day spectators. Of course, certain facilities necessary for the spectators, commercial booths available to local and area merchants and educational displays will be arranged for.

"After reading everything available about the events in Craterville in 1863, I am convinced that a most entertaining and educational docudrama around those events can be staged very successfully. Imagine the excitement of both adults and children of seeing two bodies of men in authentic Civil War uniforms draw up in battle formation facing one another. Imagine the advance in good order of one force. Then the first volley of gunfire rolls as the attackers near their opponents. This is followed by continued exchanges of musket fire from both sides. Consider the dramatized effect as the exchanges of fire result in men on both sides beginning to fall in simulation of the effects of battle. Finally, the decimated attackers retreat honorably in good order and the victors exult in their success.

"Such a battle very nearly happened here in Craterville as the union and confederate factions among the gold miners each resolved that the entire gold production of Craterville should be provided to the side they favored in the conflict raging in the East.

"As some of you may know, the only thing that prevented a battle over the gold was the acquisition by the union troops under Captain Horace Broadbent of a cannon from one of the union ships in the harbor of San Francisco. When the union gunners displayed their skill with the weapon in preparing for an imminent engagement, the confederate sympathizers disbanded their militia group and no longer resisted that all the gold mined in Craterville be shipped to San Francisco to fund the union war effort.

"What I envision is an engagement where the cannon is used after an actual exchange of gun fire. It becomes the deciding factor in the engagement as it did in the historical situation. I assure you that I have ample experience in finding the volunteer personnel and equipment for this dramatization and preparing participants, including any locals who want to participate, to act out a spirited encounter exactly as it would have occurred in 1863.

"As to the site for the event, There is a large meadow at the western edge of town which is a perfect place to perform the event. In fact, it is exactly the sort of terrain that would have been favored by the military for an engagement in those days. For your purposes, as the mayor has described them to me, this location has the additional element of being very large. The combatants, based on what I've read, would not have exceeded fifty to seventy-five men on each side. There will be ample room for parking—an essential if attracting tourists is one of the aims. Also, there will be ample room for booths for commercial enterprises, not only for the sale of goods but to sell food and beverages as well. In fact, if you wanted to add to the drawing power of the event, there would be space for a flea market, which always seems to bring a large clientele. However, you may wish to limit the opportunity for sales to your local merchants, I think you will be surprised at the revenue that local merchants will reap from this event, performed on both days of a summer weekend."

Nettleton stopped then, looking confident that he had presented an idea that would be enticing for various elements in the Craterville community. "Thank you, Mr. Nettleton," the mayor said. Turning to his colleagues on the council, he asked, "Do the members of the council have any questions of Mr. Nettleton before I invite members of the audience to participate?"

H. Lee Sampson, the school principal, put forward his hand and forearm as a request for recognition. The mayor gave him the floor and Sampson said, "Mr. Mayor, I don't understand exactly what the council is being asked to do."

The mayor failed to suppress a bit of impatience at a question he considered over-obvious. "The council is being asked to be the sponsor of the event in question," he answered with a smile meant to make up for an attitude he would have preferred to conceal.

"I anticipate that some considerable expense will be involved." Sampson persisted although he blushed timidly.

"There will be no expense to the town," Sulliband said. "A local business had agreed to provide the financial support for the event. The funding, although significant, will be less that what your might expect since Mr. Nettleton does not intend to profit from the event. You may recall I said at the outset that his is a non-profit company."

"Mr. Mayor," began Reverend Purefoy, his voice exercising its full, pulpit-level resonance. That usually indicated that a sermonette was under way. "I do not doubt the commercial potential of this scheme; however, I wonder if it is appropriate for the town to be the official sponsor of a presentation of an episode of violence, especially since some license is being taken with history to portray more violence than actually occurred. After all, perhaps the early settlers of Craterville should be judged more admirable for having rejected bloodshed rather than succumbing to it. Why should we sponsor an event that portrays them as resorting to killing when they did not?"

In their seats in the last row, Joe and Carey turned to one another and smiled wryly. Joe was sure that Carey was also thinking of the prostitution, gambling, drinking and general climate of violence which was the typical history of Gold Rush mining camps. He wondered how far Reverend Purefoy would go to argue the moral fiber of the Craterville miners, some of whom had deserted the army to pursue a dream of rapid wealth and riotous living.

Robert B. Nettleton, who was still on his feet, gestured toward the mayor to be heard and said, "If I may, Mr. Mayor." The mayor nodded his permission and Nettleton said, "I respect the gentleman's concern, but I would ask him to envision the re-enactment within the larger context of the events of its time. In organizing these events, I see to the inclusion of displays about the events and issues of the period of the War between the States. The displays will be staffed by knowledgeable presenters who elaborate on the materials shown. The educational aspects of the event will not be slighted,

I assure you. Both the issues and the great leaders of that conflict will be given their just due. Nor will the heroism of the common soldier in that war, which has never been surpassed, be slighted. Displays at the event will give the visitors a chance to be reminded of a proud yet tragic time in American history. Do not look on the mock battle as a glorification of violence but as a symbol of men fighting for a cause in which they passionately believed."

In the front row of the audience, Evan Iverson rose to his feet and began speaking with firmness ringing in his voice even before Sulliband recognized him to speak. "Mr. Mayor, what is the name of the company that is funding this event?"

The mayor maintained his placidity in responding. "The donor prefers to remain anonymous."

"Isn't it odd that a company prefers not to garner some good will from such a gesture?" Evan asked pointedly

Sulliband shrugged. "Strange or not, that is a condition of the gift."

"Don't you find it suspicious?' Even asked sharply.

Mayor merely shook his head negatively. A silence followed. The mayor looked to his left and right to see if any councilors wanted to be recognized. He looked down at his papers, obviously avoiding looking at the audience. Evan was not to be put off. "I insist that you tell the name of the company who is willing to support the event, Mr. Mayor."

"Why do you insist on knowing?" broke in Councilman Jepson, the hardware store owner.

"Because I suspect that the company in question has offered support for this project, especially at this time, because it wants to divert attention from one if its other activities that would outrage this community."

"That's ridiculous," said the mayor.

Out of the corner of his eye, Joe saw that Carey was raising her hand to be asked to speak. He grabbed her wrist and pulled her arm down as he raised his own arm for recognition. The mayor pointed to him and nodded his permission to speak. Joe got to his feet and said, "I don't see why it is necessary to have the name of the donor. If the project is worth doing, we don't need to know who is funding it. I find it refreshingly different that a company isn't trying to milk a public-spirited action for all the publicity it can get." The entire council smiled at Joe's statement. Evan Iverson turned to glare at Joe. Joe thought it prudent to say no more and sat down.

Receiving recognition from the mayor, Councilman Harrison, the forest ranger, said, "I think we're getting side-tracked here. Isn't the real question whether this event would be good for the town? I think it will be. Besides, it's not often that we can have something which will draw a lot of trade to town with no drain on the public purse."

"Doesn't the use of guilt money bother you?" Evan injected stridently.

"We don't know that," Jepson retorted. "Mayor, can you assure the council that there's no impropriety about the source of the money?"

"No impropriety whatsoever," Sullliband said tersely.

"Then I move that the town sponsor the re-enactment event," Jepson said.

Sampson muttered a second to Jepson's motion and the vote taken shortly after carried unanimously.

As the mayor moved the council on to other business, Joe decided that Evan's opportunity to set off fireworks was past and got up to go. Carey followed Joe into the vestibule and tugged him around after the door had closed behind them. She pointed an accusing finger at him and said, "I did not appreciate what you did in there."

"I thought I ought to do something to squelch Evan's ploy," Joe explained.

"I was about to do the same thing when you decided to interfere."

"Carey," Joe pleaded. "It's better that Evan be annoyed with me than you."

"Oh," she scoffed, "you think I can't handle him? Trust me; I've had fifteen years experience."

Joe smiled warmly at her. "Then you really don't need any more practice at it, do you?" He left her pondering that as he continued out the door toward his car.

20

OVER THE NEXT SEVERAL days, Joe tried to stay focused on his work. That was not easy since he was expecting an unfriendly visit at any moment from Evan Iverson. When anticipation of the unpleasantness began hampering his work, he called Carey to find out if she had any idea when the axe would fall.

"I think we can relax," Carey reported. "Evan's attention is on another matter for the moment. He's helping Jimmy Chinn get ready for the regional of the state high school track meet this Friday and Saturday and doesn't have time for anything else."

"Should I be sending a condolence card to the high school track coach that he has the pleasure of Evan at his elbow?"

"No need, really. Since the coach is familiar with Evan's career in track and field and admires him, he's actually pleased to have Evan's help. Besides, Evan's a different person around track and field training and meets. You wouldn't believe the personality change; he's full of encouragement and instruction gently delivered."

Joe asked, "With Jimmy gone, you'll be shorthanded at the store, I take it. Can I help?" The offer was his indirect means of visiting with Carey, whom he was reluctant to interact with in a purely social fashion that might be construed as romantic interest, which he tried to deny, even to himself, that it was.

"I'm covered, thank goodness," Carey said. "One of the high school girls is going to help me out."

Failing at a cover for his real intent, Joe admitted, "Actually I've been wanting to reciprocate for that delicious dinner you invited me to. Would you consider it insulting to offer you dinner at the Niner this Saturday night as adequate reciprocation?"

"You mean rather than your very own cooking?" Carey asked, playing at sounding disappointed.

"My cooking's a culinary experience you can do without, I assure you."

Carey chuckled. "You're probably being overly modest. However, I'd be delighted to accept your offer. Saturdays in the store are usually quite taxing and I'd be delighted not have to fend for myself for an evening meal."

"I know you close at six. Shall we meet at the Niner at six thirty?" Joe suggested.

"Sounds great, Joe," Carey said and added her goodbye. Joe was very pleased. Disproportionately pleased, he had to admit, for a man who had resolved that he would avoid romance for the year that he was committed to devoting himself exclusively to his writing.

Having convinced himself that he was not being over-eager but courteous to arrive at the Niner at ten minutes after six, Joe had begun his second cup of coffee when Carey came through the door. He stood and held a chair for her as she shrugged off her light jacket while approaching the table. "Am I late?" she asked.

"Right on time," Joe answered without looking at his watch. He adjusted Carey's chair behind her as she dropped into it with a sigh of relief.

"Tough day?' Joe asked.

"Saturdays are normally busy," Carey said, "but it wouldn't have been so bad if I hadn't been shorthanded."

"I thought you had some help lined up," Joe said.

"I did, but she backed out. Or, rather, her father did for her."

"Her father objected to her working?" Joe wondered.

"Oh, he doesn't mind her working," Carey explained. "It's working for me that he won't permit."

"Good God, why?"

"It's a long story," Carey said and swiveled her head from side to side to indicate that she wanted no discussion.

"I love long stories," Joe said. "I'm a writer, remember? We love long stories."

"You wouldn't like this one unless you're into horror stories," Carey grumbled. Her face showed a mixture of anger and frustration.

Joe was about to press her further, but a waitress approached to take their order, which was quickly given since they knew the restaurant's menu and which of its choices were their favorites.

When the waitress left, Joe lightly touched the back of Carey's hand with his fingers. "You look like you should talk about what's happened."

Carey turned her hand over and gave Joe's fingers a brief squeeze. "Maybe later, after dinner," she said.

Their dinners were not long in coming. Of the total of a half-dozen eating places in Craterville, there were several which offered more stylish fare. However, these restaurants that tried to appeal to the palates of the tourist trade could not match the Niner for flavorful and satisfying meals that appealed to the American palate that preferred the traditional to the exotic.   Joe and Carey ate with dedication and enjoyment. However, throughout dinner they both failed in their rather forced tries at casual conversation. The unexpressed but nagging reason for Carey's distress hovered between them, somehow short-circuiting every innocuous topic that would have added pleasantry to meals that were up to the usual enjoyable standard that made the Niner restaurant the overwhelmingly favored restaurant of choice among locals.

"Let's have coffee at my place," Carey suggested when their dinner plates had been cleared.

Joe agreed willingly. A short time later he was seated on the couch in Carey's living room as she brought a tray with the coffee and a plate of cookies out of the kitchen and set it on the coffee table before him. Joe smiled broadly at the cookies. "Carey, you really know the way to my heart. Those are the raspberry filled coconut cookies that I have to ration strictly when I buy them. Otherwise the entire package disappears on the day when I bring them into the cabin."

"You don't need to restrain yourself tonight," Carey said as she settled into a chair facing him across the coffee table.

The coffee and cookies consumed the couple's attention longer than ought to have been the case until Joe said, "Are you ready to tell me what happened that causes some local father to prohibit his daughter's clerking in your store?"

Carey sighed and poured herself some more coffee. After continuing to look into her cup as though for some avenue of escape, she finally said, "I helped his daughter out of a jam a few weeks ago, and he just found out about it. He doesn't appreciate my helping her. When he found out she had agreed to work today, he stormed in to tell me that his daughter would not be working for me today or any other day."

Joe uttered a little gasp of surprise. "That's strange behavior toward someone for the person's helping out your kid."

"Not only can't she work for me, he threatened dire consequences if I so much as talked to the girl ever again."

"What's this guy? The village nut case?"

"Hardly. He happens to be the very reverend Mr. Billy Purefoy," Carey grumbled with anything but respect.

"The minister who's on the town council?"

Carey nodded. "He's the one."

"What's his problem?' Joe's feelings about Carey being what they were, he was immediately annoyed on her behalf. He could not imagine anything she could have done that would be unacceptable to a rational person.

Carey took a long time to answer. When she did, she began with obvious reluctance. "Remember the day you were in my apartment and a high school girl came up to see me?"

Joe grinned. "And you had me get a box of candy out of the safe? How could I forget it? I never saw such a big deal made out of buying a little box of candy in my life."

"Well," Carey sighed and shrugged. "These are a special kind of candy. You might say that they are real life savers for the consumers who need them."

Joe was puzzled by Carey's apparent gravity. "They must be the flavor of the century to merit being stored in a safe."

"As you might suspect," Carey said facing Joe squarely, "they are not candy at all. I keep them in candy wrappers to make them less obvious to anyone but the girl who's going to use them."

"The 'them' in this case is what?"

"Birth control pills. In this case, the so-called morning-after pills."

It took a moment before Joe grasped what Carey had said. "You mean the pills someone takes after sex to avoid pregnancy?"

"Yes."

"You sell them?' Joe wondered.

"No. I give them away."

"How do the girls know to come to you?"

"Word of mouth."

Joe was not shocked but was rather amazed that Carey could provide such a service in a small town the size of Craterville and there not be a public controversy, let alone demands for the law to come down on Carey. "Carey, you're taking a terrible risk."

"It's my position that those pills should be available to anyone who wants then, Joe. It isn't coincidence that I keep them in wrappers that say *Yours to Choose.* I believe that's what they are. If I can prevent some girl's entire life being shaped by an hour or two of recklessness, it's worth the risk."

"Good God, woman, how long do you think this can go on?" Joe asked with some exasperation. "Talk about a life being shaped by a brief incident, how about yours? How long do you think your open secret will last now that a fundamentalist minister knows and thinks you've wronged his daughter?"

"I doubt the reverend will be a problem. He can't go public about me without embarrassing his daughter, whose behavior he really sees as a personal embarrassment." Joe was astonished at Carey's aplomb as she continued, "I doubt he's the first parent in town who's found out that a daughter got that special candy from me. In fact, I suspect a few girls didn't get them for personal use but for their mothers." In any case, the availability of the medicine is not something that anyone wants to go public with. The hypocrites would be embarrassed to have the use of the pills by someone in the family be known, and those who approve don't want to stop the medicine's being available in case someone they care about needs it in the future. I have kept very complete records, and I have made it known that I will make them public if I get in a jam."

Joe could not help but enjoy the deliciousness of the situation over Carey's pregnancy choice program. Carey and Craterville were happily holding each other hostage. That would be a deplorable situation if Carey were taking advantage, or if the service she was providing had a harmful result. At some risk to herself, Carey was a benevolent benefactor of the community, even if it pained some members of the community to accept that benevolence. On the other hand, he would rather that a woman that he liked and admired not be in a precarious position, notwithstanding her conviction that circumstances were sufficient protection. Otherwise, he found the situation so vastly amusing that it would be hard to resist the temptation to fictionalize it.

"You're foolish to take such a risk," Joe felt compelled to say.

"I'm not worried, Joe. I am annoyed that Honor Purefoy, who is a genuinely nice kid, is being put through a bad time by her father."

"She shouldn't have let him find out," Joe grumbled. "Either she admitted to her father out of guilt that she'd taken the pill, or she told someone who got the information back to the good reverend. Either way, she's responsible for her own discomfort. But what's new about a human being making life hard for him or her self?" Joe concluded wryly.

The discussion of the matter being somehow concluded by Joe's statement, the pair devoted themselves to the cookies and coffee for a time, although Joe did not feel as sanguine that Carey faced no danger to continue the help she gave unwed, possibly pregnant girls as she did. When it came time for him to go, Joe said, "I'll come in to give you a hand in the store tomorrow."

"No, you won't," Carey said emphatically. "I know you write every day, and I won't have you disrupting your schedule to become a grocery clerk."

"Come on, Carey. I know that the time of year has come when your weekend traffic in the store begins to pick up as the cabin owners start coming for weekends and the day trippers start to appear. It won't hurt me to give you a little help."

"Not necessary, Joe. Really," Carey insisted. "I'll get on the phone this evening and find someone to give me a few hours tomorrow."

"I'm coming in," Joe said. "So save your breath."

Carey looked like she was trying to be annoyed and could not manage it. "You're determined to be obstreperous, aren't you?" She sighed resignedly. "O.K., you can come in at one o'clock, if you'll swear you're going to put in at least three hours writing tomorrow morning."

Joe grinned and gave an affirmative nod. "Swearing is something I'll be doing anyway if the words don't come. You're sure that one o'clock is soon enough?"

"It actually is," Carey said. "Things don't get really busy until the afternoon."

"All right, I'll see you then," Joe said. He gave Carey the briefest of pecks on the cheek and left her apartment. On the short drive home, his mind kept returning to his parting gesture. He had never kissed Carey before, not even with a fleeting peck like the one he had just given her. He had kissed her without any forethought. Had it been a mistake?

The next day, he was just sitting down over a sandwich after a full morning's work when Carey phoned him. "I've got help for this afternoon, Joe. So you needn't spoil your day by coming in."

"You're kidding me," Joe said. Perhaps she had decided to forego his help simply to avoid his presence. That would mean his kissing her, as platonic as it had been, had been a mistake.

"No, really," Carey assured him warmly. "I've got help. Experienced help and newly pedigreed help at that."

"What's that mean?"

"I happen to have the regional high school decathlon champion working the checkout as we speak," Carey said with sunniness in her tone that seemed genuine.

"Jimmy Chinn won at the regional track meet," Joe inferred immediately.

"Yes, isn't it wonderful?"

Joe was pleased. "I suppose Evan's basking in reflected glory."

"Actually, he hasn't been in," Carey said. "Jimmy says he's busy helping the high school track coach prepare to field scholarship offers."

"I'm delighted for Jimmy. It's great to see a good kid get ahead, isn't it?" Joe said sincerely. "You're sure you don't need me?" he asked.

"I'm sure."

"Offer congratulations to Jimmy for me," Joe asked.

"Will do, Joe. See you soon," Carey concluded.

The pleasant tone in Carey's voice was reassuring, Joe decided. He looked forward to a pleasant afternoon secure that his most cherished friendship was intact.

21

JOE VENTURED INTO TOWN only twice in the next few weeks. The advance of spring into early summer made the forest around the cabin, which he thought could not possibly become more attractive, even more irresistible for long walks and interludes of tranquil reverie. Also, he liked what he was writing. A story was actually taking shape, one that he rather liked. Working was easy and began each day without procrastination nor ended soon after starting at the first opportunity offered by rationalization.

On the coming weekend, the now well-publicized re-enactment of the so-called Battle of Craterville was to occur on each day of the weekend. Many local residents were drawn to the site of the re-enactment as the preparatory activity began to take place several days before the event. Joe could not resist driving by for his own glance at the work. On the nearer-to-town edge of the large meadow, a pattern of stakes appeared which, it was explained to anyone who inquired, laid out the parking area and the place where a row of booths would be raised for the sale of a variety of merchandise and for educational displays. Local merchants had been invited to apply to rent booths for varying amounts depending on the perceived choiceness of the locations within the pattern prescribed for separating the food and drink sellers from the vendors of a variety of other merchandise ranging from clothing, souvenirs, and facsimile Civil War artifacts. The purveyors of these latter items were out-of-town sellers whose business it was to travel from one of these re-enactments to another throughout the summer. To be sure of establishing amicable relations with the local merchants, the event organizer gave locals preferential consideration when the applications for space out-distanced the available space. The exceptions were those exhibitors, all of them outsiders, who were providing so-called educational displays.

Joe was not even certain that he would bother to view the re-enactment itself. However, because he had agreed to assist Carey with her business participation in the event, he could with little effort see the mock battle on either day. Carey had applied for a booth in which she intended to sell sandwiches and a variety of non-alcoholic beverages. Because local residents found the lure of attending as spectators so irresistible, she was having difficulty finding workers to assist her both to prepare for the selling and to man the booth during the noon-to-dusk hours of the two day event. She asked Joe to help her augment the slender work force consisting of herself and Jimmy Chinn and. for the preparation phase of each day, two of the local ladies who occasionally assisted her in the store.

Carey had emphasized for Joe that he would be unwelcome before the afternoon of each day of the re-enactment weekend so that she could be certain that helping her had not interfered with his work. Joe asked if a sworn affidavit that he had worked prior to arriving would be necessary. Carey responded that, since she had not thought of that requirement herself, it would be unnecessary this time. However, she would keep it in mind for future instances if she sought help. Joe was secretly pleased at the indication that there would be future instances.

When Joe did arrive at the event site at one o'clock on Saturday, he was astonished by the scene which presented itself to him.

Several orange vested attendants were using every last bit of the designated parking area to squeeze in late arriving vehicles. There were several hundred cars parked in close proximity to one another behind the display and vending booths, which extended the entire length of the parking area and faced it. Behind the booths, hundreds of spectators sat, stood or milled around in a strip which was roped off from what would be the battleground. Neither cars, concessions, nor people encroached on this open space which ran from the highway west out of Craterville to the Miwok River, which paralleled the road, and beyond. The portion of the meadow across the river from the larger expanse adjacent to the highway was a fifty foot wide piece that lay in front of the steep assent of the mountain slope. In this parcel, as at the opposite end bordering the road, a dozen tents had been erected. No uniformed re-enactors were in evidence at the moment. Joe knew from the publicity that the battle enactment itself was still two hours away.

Having had to park at the very periphery of the lot near the highway, Joe walked down the line of booths in search of Carey's stand. He passed a succession of clothing and souvenir stands before he arrived at a line of food-vending booths. He admired the logic of having placed this essential commodity centrally. Joe spotted the sign over the booth which read, Craterville Grocery: Sandwiches and Beverages. As he walked up to the stand, Carey was handing a customer a bag of purchases and some change. In response to his greeting, Carey smiled with relief and sighed, "Am I ever glad to see you."

"Well, a guy always loves to be appreciated," Joe grinned. Then, observing that Carey was alone, he asked, "Where's your help? Surely not out to lunch rather than having a sandwich here?"

"The ladies who helped me this morning have been gone for an hour and Jimmy didn't show," Carey said with a long face.

"I thought he was your most reliable help."

Carey nodded affirmatively. "He is normally. Some kind of family emergency. A friend of his stopped by to tell me a couple hours ago. I hope you're really serious about helping." She walked to the counter to assist a couple with two children who were discussing whether to buy ready-made sandwiches visible in the cooler or having Carey make them some fresh. The children opted for hot dogs from the enclosed grilling unit that displayed them as they cooked on heated, rotating rods. The parents asked Carey to make two turkey sandwiches on whole wheat bread. While she prepared the order, Joe stood at Carey's elbow and observed, "I'm going to need some instruction in sandwich-making if I'm going to be any real help."

"Actually it would be an incredible help if you took orders, got beverages from the cooler and tended the register, I'll make sandwiches and tell you the total of the orders. That should get us through O.K."

In response to Joe's nod of assent, Carey squeezed his bicep and smiled appreciatively. In a few minutes, they developed a rhythm and an efficiency to their functioning. They even managed to work with good humor even though business became increasingly rushed as hunger and thirst registered with the spectators who had arrived some time ago and had already done their share of wandering and shopping.

As the time for the battle re-enactment neared, Joe and Carey sighed with relief as the number of buyers diminished to a few rushing to get a ready-make sandwich or a cold beverage before they hurried to find a location from which to view the re-enactment.

Shortly before three o'clock, Evan Iverson strode purposefully up to the stand and asked where Jimmy Chinn was. When informed that an emergency had kept him from coming to work, Evan's concern arose immediately. He had planned to discuss with Jimmy this afternoon the eight most promising scholarship offers that the high school track coach had received for the boy. Evan's main concern was that the emergency that had kept Jimmy away might be some physical injury. When Carey could not provide information on the specifics of the emergency, Evan mumbled in frustration and started toward the parking lot. Carey asked Evan if he was not going to watch the mock battle that was about to begin.

Evan re-approached the counter of the booth and said too softly to be heard widely, "After having been exposed to the theme of the so-called educational display in the booth sponsored by the Daughters of the Confederacy, I'd only watch if the union side were going to use live ammunition." With a dismissive wave of his hand, he disappeared between the first row of parked cars.

Carey looked at Joe with an amused expression, "Always consistent, isn't he?' How about you, Joe? Aren't you going to watch?"

"If you don't mind my deserting you," Joe confessed.

"As you can see, I won't have any trouble handling things now. I hope you will come back after its over. We should get a rush then."

Assuring Carey he would return immediately after the performance, Joe hastened to see if he could find a good spot from which to view the mock battle. He soon found that the viewing strip was lined in its entirety with a closely packed crowd which was six or seven people deep. Fortunately he was able to find a spot to stand where those in front of him were either seated on the ground or short enough when standing to see over.

The considerable noise of conversation and the restlessness of some spectators made Joe hope that the event would start on time.

He spent his time studying his fellow spectators and was interested in the wide variety of people who had been drawn to the unusual event. Joe was charmed with the efforts of a mother who was patiently trying to keep three energetic and restless children under control while her oblivious husband was absorbed in whatever he was reading.

Suddenly the noise stopped as the sound of drums beating at a marching tempo was heard to the right and behind the spectators. The adults turned toward the highway and the sound of drums and marchers approaching from behind them. Some children ducked under the rope boundary and prepared to scramble toward the sound until alert parents pulled them behind the rope marking off the viewing area.

Shortly, a column of men in dark blue Civil War vintage uniforms marching four abreast appeared on the highway preceded by two drummers. When they were parallel to the clear portion of the meadow just past the viewing area, they responded to a sharply stated command given by someone on the far side of the column and turned the column in good order into the meadow. They marched past the tents to a point midway between the tents and the river before they were ordered to halt. On command, they wheeled into a single line, stopped, lowered their muskets to their sides, and remained at attention. There were sixty men in the line, some whose trim bodies conveyed a military bearing and others whose bulging waistlines prevented a soldierly image. The soldier-performers stood rigidly as three officers walked the length of the line and inspected their troop. When the officers had completed their inspection, the three returned to the center of the line and faced their troop. One of the three stepped forward, turned to salute the other two and then turned again to the troop. He gave a command and the unit wheeled back into a column of fours and the men marched toward the spectators.

For the next ten minutes the officer put the troop through a series of marching maneuvers executed with surprising precision. Finally he marched them directly toward the crowd and halted them about twenty feet away. He ordered them into two rows facing the spectators. Upon command, the front row knelt on one knee while the second rank remained standing behind them. Another command made the blue-clad force load their weapons.

For those like Joe, who had not seen the leaflet that described the sequence of events to occur, which many in the crowd held in their hands, there was a moment of concern until the knowledgeable persons among them spread the word that the actors had loaded powder but no balls into the guns. Another command was issued and the soldiers leveled their guns at the crowd. On order, the front rank fired their guns. The spectators gasped, not withstanding assurances from their informed neighbors that the guns were not loaded. As the crowd calmed from its moment of fear and excitement and began to chuckle about their previous apprehension, a second volley came their way from the second row of troops. The audience responded with immediate pleasure this time.

As the audience clapped and conversed animatedly, the union force was then ordered back into a column of fours and marched to the center of the meadow. The officer formed them into a single line, surveyed them briefly and then dismissed the troop, The men relaxed and began to saunter toward their tents. Some sat on the ground outside the tents and others moved about purposefully. Soon fires were burning and the smell of brewing coffee was in the air.

No sooner was the blue-clad union contingent settled into their tented camp when a trumpet was heard from the direction of the tents on the far side of the river at the opposite end of the meadow from the union camp. Men dressed in the gray uniforms of the Confederacy began to scramble out of the tents across the river where they had gone unnoticed by Joe and apparently most of the other spectators until now. With much bustle they formed themselves into a single line facing across the meadow toward the union tents. Their number was similar to that of the union force. Soon they were inspected by their own three officers. Afterward, they were ordered into a column of fours and were marched down to the river bank. Since the stream was only knee-deep and flowing gently, as was normal for this time of year, the column soon had crossed it and come to the center of the meadow where the union force had drilled a few moments earlier.

The gray-clad soldiers executed their own set of maneuvers until the officer brought them to a halt in the center of the meadow in a single line facing the spectators. They remained at attention briefly about fifty yards from the crowd. The soldiers were then ordered to fix bayonets. The spectators who had read the leaflet, mindful of the surprise that had distressed some of the spectators during the actions of the union troop, hastened to warn their neighbors that they were about to see a bayonet charge. The warning was indeed fortunate, since even foreknowledge of the sudden action did not prevent the astonishment of the crowd when the gray-clad force charged toward them. A high-pitched, sustained yell came from the closely packed line of gray uniforms as it rushed pell-mell toward the spectators. As anyone with even the least bit of acquaintance with Civil War history knew, the unnerving sound was intended to re-create the renowned rebel yell that had proven so disconcerting to union troops during the war.

If the blood-curdling sound which continued throughout the charge was anything close to what the war cry had actually been, Joe--and he was certain others in the crowd--could understand why it had caused such fear during the actual battles. As the gray wave preceded by the leveled bayonets approached the viewing area, the spectators in the front of the crowded space shrank back despite their knowledge that there was no actual danger. Joe and the others in the back rank of viewers were pressed back against the canvas walls of the concession booths by the reaction of those in front and struggled to maintain their balance.

The charge ended with the closest of the gray-clad soldiers braced with bayonets extended about six feet from the crowd of spectators. Their bayonets, which looked unnervingly authentic, remained leveled at the crowd. Total silence ensued as all motion stopped. It must have lasted only ten seconds but seemed much longer to Joe. Then the sounds of relief among the crowd began, followed soon by excited talking and finally a good deal of laughter. The rebels were called to form up in a column of fours and began to march back toward the center of the meadow. A few in the crowd began to applaud and soon a loud and extensive accolade of clapping followed the gray-clad soldiers back to the center of the meadow.

While the rebel column continued across the meadow away from the crowd, the rumble of drums brought the union soldiers back into line. Soon they were marched toward the center of the meadow and renewed their own drill while the gray force did an about face at the far side of the meadow and began to return toward the center of the open space. As the two groups continued their drills, it was inevitable that they should get in each other's way. Before long, the four-abreast column of gray uniforms was marching directly toward the blues, who had just been commanded into a single line standing at attention. It looked for a moment that a collision was imminent until the rebel officer called a halt. Another order to the gray force quickly followed and in short order the two lines of soldiers stood confronting one another at a separation of about twenty yards in parallel lines perpendicular to the spectator viewing area.

The two trios of officers strode to the middle the twenty-yard wide space between the opposing arrays and began a dialogue obviously intended to decide which unit would clear the field for the other group to continue its drill. The crowd could not hear the exchange of statements, but the accompanying gestures and body language made clear that neither set of officers was willing to yield the drill ground to their opponents. The exchanges visibly appeared to become more heated. Then one officer from each force confronted each other, their chests thrusting out in near contact.

Shortly, it appeared that cooler heads clad in both colors prevailed and an agreement appeared to be struck.

Both commanders ordered an about face and the opposing two lines marched in opposite directions, the rebels toward the river and the unionists toward their tents near the highway. Both groups stopped short as they approached the obstacles. Neither group did an about face, but both commands were ordered into the two line firing formation earlier exhibited by the union force. With their backs to each other, each force fired a practice volley, which would have been harmless even as a real event with live ammunition. However, when each group discharged a second volley, one of the soldiers in the gray-clad force fell to the ground as though shot. The rebels acted out a brief period of noisy confusion. Then, appearing to have concluded that one of the union soldiers had fired into their backs, the rebels berated their attackers verbally until they were ordered into a double line facing their opponents. They quickly loaded their weapons and sent a pair of volleys toward the union soldiers, who had turned in response to the sounds of anger expressed behind them. Six or seven of the union actors fell to the ground as though shot.

After some confusion, the union force came to order and formed their double line facing the grays. In quick succession, they released a pair of volleys at the rebels. Then an exchange of disciplined fire began that lasted through several minutes during which men dropped on both sides. Then the rebels were ordered to fix bayonets. The order to move forward was given and the rebels began to march at a measured pace toward the blue force. It appeared that a few of the union soldiers broke ranks and were about to flee in the face of the bayonet charge which had not yet broken into a run toward them. However, what the unionists were now seen to do was open the side of the largest of their tents, revealing a cannon which had been hidden inside. The detachment which had broken rank quickly moved the gun to the union line, which opened to let the gun be placed in firing position. The advancing rebel force had just broken into a run toward the union force when the first shot from the cannon was fired. Nearly a dozen of the attackers fell to the ground. As the cannon was being reloaded, blue troops randomly fired at the rebels. A second discharge of the cannon further devastated the rebels, who had now lost at least half of their original number. The remaining attackers stopped their forward movement and fired sporadically at the union soldiers until the rebel officers ordered a retreat.

The badly depleted rebel force hastened back to the river, where it took cover along the river bank and began to return the union fire with good effect. The blue fire, both from muskets and the cannon, was ineffective against the now protected gray force. The union officers organized their men in a line to attack. When they advanced to the middle of the meadow, a now well concentrated rebel fire resulted in a considerable number of casualties. The remaining unionists retreated to their position near the cannon. Crouching for cover as best they could, the blue coats kept up a fire toward the river bank. After a five minute continuation of sporadic fire, it became apparent that the more exposed union force was taking more casualties. However, the rebels could not leave their protected position along the river back for fear of the damage the union's cannon would do.

Both sides simultaneously showed a flag of truce. The officers for each force strode to the center of the meadow now littered with the still forms of the supposed casualties. Very briefly, a truce was agreed to. After gathering up their casualties, the union officers marched their band back onto the highway from which they came. The rebels picked up their fallen men and formed up along the river bank. They marched in the opposite direction of the unionists until they disappeared into the wooded area at the end of the meadow. The meadow was now as empty as it had been before the battle re-enactment began. After a brief silence, the spectators began to applaud and cheer enthusiastically.

Joe joined in the clapping. He reflected with some amusement that the performance had indeed been entertaining. He had been wondering all week as the preparations went on how the re-enactors would achieve an exciting re-enactment of a battle that had never taken place. Like anyone who had lived in Craterville for even a brief length of time, he knew the history of the town in the Civil War period. Confederate and union factions had organized and prepared for an engagement in the hopes of prevailing in their desire to have the gold from the then-lucrative strike shipped to the government to which they owed allegiance. However, before any engagement occurred, the acquisition of a cannon by the union force made the rebel sympathizers wisely concede in the struggle to control the destination of the gold. Joe could see that a plausible embroidery of the historical reality had been the basis for the mock battle presented.

Of course, the hypothetical battle did require for its engendering an act of treachery on the part of the union sympathizers. Joe recalled the state of annoyance in which Evan Iverson had left before the performance. Did he know that the unionists were going to be portrayed as treacherous and refused to stay and watch because of that? How would Evan have known that union treachery was going to be the event that triggered the imagined battle? Perhaps a display among the so-called educational exhibits had given him a clue. Joe decided that when Carey no longer needed his help at her booth, he would view those exhibits and see if something was being presented that had triggered Evan's distress.

Joe got back to Carey's booth about the same time a pack of eager customers arrived to quench the thirsts that had grown while they watched the performance. He and Carey worked feverishly for about a half hour before business slacked off. The crowd was in high spirits after watching the dramatic re-creation of a supposed

Civil War engagement and seemed interested in roaming about exploring the exhibits of facsimile memorabilia as well as the wide range of clothing, collectibles and other merchandise that had no connection to Civil War history but were typical commercial additions to re-enactment events around the country.

When the frequency of customers declined to a number that Carey could handle alone, Joe asked if he could join the milling crowd to explore the booths before the late afternoon brought another surge of hungry re-enactment buffs to Carey's sandwich shop. Carey asked if Joe would return in an hour so that she could satisfy her own curiosity about the vending aspect of the event before the final business rush. Joe promised to return and left in search of the so-called educational displays where he might get some insight into Evan Iverson's dismay over what he had encountered there.

The educational booths were grouped together at the very end of the line of canvas structures. The booth devoted to great military commanders of the Civil War drew his attention first. The array was quite legitimately interesting. It was devoted to the who and what of military leadership on both sides of the conflict. While there was a bit more space and glamour accorded to several Confederate commanders whose careers were well known for effectiveness and daring, the presentation seemed balanced to Joe since tradition had not identified counterparts of similar dash on the Union side. It was a slight surprise to find President Lincoln and Jefferson Davis accorded similar space and gravity in the exhibit; however, this was not a total novelty to Joe, who had visited Gettysburg once and noted the considerable recognition given the leader of the rebellious states.

Joe found the largest booth, which was devoted to major battles of the war, very informative through its use of photographs and models of terrain with indicators of troop placements. He would have spent more time reading the labeling and explanatory placards had this booth not been the most crowded. The booth devoted to California's role in the war was devoted mostly to the political, technological and financial matters which were relevant to the struggle in the east. Although California had not been a location where extensive fighting had occurred, many Californians had served in the war. In recognition of this fact, a map indicating the location of veterans' graveyards was featured.

Joe almost missed the booth arranged by the Daughters of the Confederacy. It was not only the last one in the entire line of booths but also fronted in a ninety degree direction from the others. A perusal of the few displays in this booth revealed to Joe that here was the place where Evan Iverson in all likelihood had found what he had considered a very distasteful presentation. The sole goal of the several displays was to interpret for the viewer the political and social issues that led to the struggle to dissolve or preserve the union.

The central political point asserted was that the war was not about slavery at all, but was a conflict over states' rights. A concise display consisting of brief text and photographs of John C. Calhoun, Jefferson Davis, Stephen A. Douglas and a few less well-known figures traced the decades of argument over the right of individual states to live by their own legislation or social practices that were in conflict with federal law.

The specific social practice at issue between the states and the federal government was placed within the broader context of a state's right to choose its own life style so that slavery seemed a defensible matter of freedom of choice. Even that it meant the freedom to own people was hence reduced by context. Citing the fact that less than twenty percent of southerners owned slaves, the argument was made that the preservation of the institution of slavery could not have been paramount in the minds of the majority of southerners who fought for or supported the secessionist cause. He noted a placard conveying the statement by a cabinet member in a recent federal administration asserting that too much was lost on behalf of states rights by the south's losing the Civil War.

It was asserted through another much briefer display that, except for a few exceptions, the life of slaves was not so bad. Most slaves were happy, it was stated. The interpretation that was given to the events presented in Harriet Beecher Stowe's famous fictional account of slave life, which had done so much to outrage northerners' sentiments at the time was to call it an extreme and blatant piece of propaganda.

The third exhibit was a collection of books for sale. The non-fiction ones, judged by the titles and their fly leaves, were devoted to sympathetic treatments of the southern cause in the Civil War or to the biographies of southern leaders and heroes. The books of fiction appeared to tell stories of southern bravery or success during the conflict.

Joe imagined that his reaction to the displays was not much different than Iverson's had been. He believed that the states rights exhibit amounted to a reprehensible whitewash. After all, one had to ignore the historical fact that the one right that slave states asserted must continue was the use of slaves. Joe had looked to see if there was any mention of the wrangling preceding the war over having new states added to the union in equal numbers on both sides of the slavery question so that a voting majority in congress that would legislate the end of slavery could be avoided. There was nothing about the decades of political controversy preceding the actual conflict.

Joe recognized that the effort to assert that slave life was not so bad was even more reprehensible than the states rights argument. The documentation of barbaric physical punishment and sexual abuse was too extensive and well known for any reasonable person to take an assertion of tolerable slave life seriously.

Joe was fully convinced that Evan Iverson's visit to this booth had been the reason for his annoyance with the day's re-enactment event. He could imagine the intensity of Evan's reaction if he had stayed to see that the spark for an imagined Battle of Craterville had been an act of unionist treachery. Eager to conclude his exposure to the distasteful presentations, Joe returned to assist Carey with her task for the remainder of the day.

22

THE NEXT MORNING, JOE cut short his usual amount of writing time so that he could get to the site of Craterville's big tourist weekend to provide Carey as much assistance as possible during a day that would match or exceed the previous day's heavy customer traffic. He was surprised at how little parking space was left although he arrived at least two hours earlier than the day before and not more than two hours after the business stands had opened. Unless there was an unlikely unfavorable turn in the weather, which he was certain neither Carey nor the other merchants wanted, Carey was in for a frantic though profitable day. The cloudless blue sky and the prospect of a sunny, balmy summer day in the mountains no doubt would maximize a large crowd of weekend visitors, summer cabin occupants and locals as well.

Carey was surprised at his early arrival but appreciative since she and the two ladies who occasionally helped her in the store or her apartment were busy providing cold drinks and an occasional sandwich to the early arrivals already grown parched or hungry in the warm sun. She was pleased to have an extra pair of hands to help prepare and wrap the sandwiches that would be purchased by those customers who did not want to take the time to have one made for them when they came to the booth. Joe worked rapidly after a bit of instruction on sandwich construction and wrapping, but the four of them still were pressed to keep up with the surprisingly heavy volume of business so early in the day. Carey pointed out to Joe that the Sunday morning edition of the Santa Clara paper had carried a rather glowing article about the previous day's activities at Craterville's big weekend. This favorable exposure plus the sparkling weather and the beginning of the summer vacation season were all contributing to what promised to be a day that would please the merchants and the attending crowd alike.

The height of the lunch time trade became a frenzy the likes of which Joe had never worked through before. Fortunately, Carey prevailed on the two ladies to delay their departure until a half-hour before the three o'clock start of the mock battle. Still, with him and the two ladies working frantically and Carey continuously tending the register to handle transactions with a rapidity and accuracy that Joe found astonishing, they were almost overwhelmed with the pace of activity. The most surprising thing to Joe was the spirit of good humor that they managed to maintain throughout their labors. In fact, the frequency of their laughter over absurd little confusions, spills and near disasters made the whole time more enjoyable than one would have imagined in advance.

When the time for the battle re-enactment neared and the customer traffic declined suddenly to near nothing, Carey paid the two ladies who had worked so effectively and sent them off with profuse thanks for their labors. Joe suggested to Carey that she should absent herself as well and see the battle dramatization that she had not had the opportunity to observe yesterday. It took some insistence on his part, but he prevailed by pointing out that she would be at a disadvantage in dialogue on the subject that was sure to dominate conversation in Craterville for the next several weeks if she did not see the mock battle. Confessing to a modicum of curiosity about the event anyway, Carey decided that she would go watch it. Joe urged that she leave immediately for the viewing area and be sure to get the descriptive leaflet in advance of the event so that she would not be taken aback by some of the actions that would occur.

After the sound of the drums signaled that the dramatization of the hypothetical Battle of Craterville had begun, Joe himself spent a rather leisurely half-hour filling the requests of a few customers who apparently had no interest in the mock battle. He remembered that he had not eaten since a rather early breakfast and ate a rather hearty lunch now that the constant need to work had ended. Joe could hear the noises of the re-enactment and the reactions of the crowd and could infer what part of the engagement was then occurring. He recognized the point where the noise of the mock battle reached its height because of the booming of cannon fire. Joe was surprised to hear a the crowd reaction different than anything that he recalled from the previous day. He heard a loud and sustained period of raucous laughter. Following the laughter came an outburst of cheering from the crowd that was impressively long and loud.

When the sound returned to the normal crowd buzz, Joe assumed that the re-enactment had concluded, but he was puzzled that the crowd did not immediately begin to filter between the canvas booths and rush for food or to explore the booths for merchandise as they had the previous day. Carey, however, shortly reappeared to help with the anticipated increase of trade.

She was wide-eyed and smiling broadly when she came into the booth. "Now that was what I call a dramatic finish," she enthused. "It wasn't mentioned in the leaflet and at first I assumed that you didn't tell me about it because you didn't want to spoil the surprise. Then I heard some people who had seen yesterday's battle say that it hadn't ended that way yesterday."

Joe was intrigued by her statement. He recalled the ending of the mock battle as somewhat muted, a stalemate suitable to the historical reality that a battle almost occurred but was averted. In fact, he had found the ending of the mock engagement anti-climactic but perhaps the most appropriate one.

"If they didn't use the finish stated in the leaflet," he frowned. "How did the battle end?"

"Well," Carey began, her eyes sparkling with amusement. "You remember the part where the union soldiers brought out their cannon and fired a few rounds, causing the confederates to retreat to the river bank?" Joe nodded affirmatively. "After that happened, a short period of trading of rifle shots and a couple cannon discharges occurred. Then, the next cannon discharge produced an explosion on the opposite bank of the river from where the rebels were crouched. A brief pause occurred, during which the union gunners seemed as confused about the explosion across the river as the rebels who had begun to yell about it. Then there were four or five more explosions on the far river bank in close succession, and the rebels came flying up out of the near bank yelling in panic, flinging their rifles away and running toward the woods on the side of the meadow away from the crowd. They looked so scared that it struck the crowd as funny, especially when it became obvious that none of them had been injured.

"As the crowd laughed, there was one final large boom and a burst of sparkling colors in the shape of an American flag appeared in the air. You've seen such a display, I'm sure, Joe, as part of the fireworks at a Fourth of July celebration. There it was, a sparkling red, white and blue flag in the cloudless sky. The crowd began to clap and cheer wildly. It was one of the wildest things I've ever seen."

The panic of the rebel soldiers did sound funny to Joe as Carey had told it. He smiled broadly. "It must have been funny, especially if it was apparent that the rebel re-enactors were unhurt and their fright was genuine. I imagine that the puzzlement of the union re-enactors was just as funny, though I don't suppose anyone noticed it."

"Oh, it was noticed and enjoyed, all right, especially after the rebels had disappeared into the woods and the unionists milled around in confusion," Carey assured him with continued amusement.

"I wonder why they did it? Changed the ending, I mean," Joe mused.

Carey shook her head from side to side. "It couldn't have been planned, not the way that the participants looked so surprised."

"Maybe the participants are just good actors who have used this ending before," Joe speculated.

"Nobody's that good an actor. They were really scared," Carey disagreed. "Besides, the reactions of the two groups struck the crowd differently. The union looked confused, but the confederates actually were made to look bad. I can't believe men would participate to look so laughable. It wasn't comedy, Joe; it was humiliation."

Joe tried another speculation. "Maybe embarrassing the rebels was to make up for making the unionists look treacherous for shooting someone in the back to start the battle."

"Then what sort of statement do you take the American flag at the end to be?"

Joe smiled, "It kind of shows a bias toward one side, doesn't it?"

"Strange, isn't it? In planning the presentation of a battle that is only hypothetical. You'd think that they'd go for an ending that made all the spectators happy with both sets of participants. Many people today still have strong feelings about that war; you'd think a Civil War fantasy would avoid enflaming either group of sympathizers," Carey offered, trying to shed her amusement for the moment.

"Of course the ending they used yesterday made one side look much less honorable than the other," Joe reflected. "Yesterday's ending was implicitly favorable to one side as to the cause of the conflict. Maybe the planners of that ending are some of those true believers who still refer to the effort for southern separatism as the glorious lost cause."

With a look of realization suddenly lighting her face, Carey asked, "You don't suppose that some spectator with a union bias about the war took the back shooting so amiss that he arranged his own ending for today, do you?"

Joe's face brightened with a similar realization. "You mean someone who was so annoyed that he would say afterward that he'd only watch the re-enactment again if the union were using live ammunition?"

"That person would have to be someone prone to extreme actions in expressing his views," Carey offered with a kind of despairing blandness coming into her expression.

"Do we know anyone like that?" Joe asked with a roll of his eyes.

At this point neither of them could restrain a laugh.

Carey stifled her laughter briefly to ask, "You think Evan the Unholy Boulder Roller has struck again?"

"Ask yourself," Joe mused aloud, "how many people do you know who have the passionate feelings and the technical know how to do something like those well-timed explosions and the fireworks display, while being careful to avoid injury to anyone?"

Carey scrunched her face unhappily as it reddened. "That idiot. Couldn't you just strangle him."

Joe's shoulders shook with laughter. "No. Not for this one, I couldn't."

"Oh, Joe, don't tell me you approve?" Carey chided and frowned in disbelief.

"Well, Carey, to be honest, I didn't react well to making the unionists stoop to treachery to touch off the battle. Here the participants are dramatizing an event that didn't even happen, and they make the union side out as the bad guys."

Carey looked at Joe with an expression of disapproval similar to the one his least favorite elementary school teacher always used to cow him completely. "That war happened a hundred fifty years ago, Joe."

"Yeh, well, tell that to the Daughters of the Confederacy," Joe said with contempt in his voice when he uttered the name of the group.

"Who?' Carey asked with genuine puzzlement.

With a gesture like an umpire calling a base runner out, Joe said, "They have a booth down the way with exhibits that justify the southern position in the Civil War with some slippery reasoning."

"What kind of exhibits?"

Joe was only too ready to launch a specific tirade on the offensive aspects of the exhibits in the booth in question when the first few spectators to break away from the buzzing about the mock battle arrived to request refreshments. For the next three hours, Joe and Carey were so busy that they could not discuss anything other than whether the sliced meats, bread and other foodstuffs would last long enough to assuage the hunger of the crowd that had come for the final day of Craterville's big weekend. Eventually, the flow of customers diminished to only the habitual fanatic shoppers who had delayed eating until their thirst for acquisition of memorabilia clashed with the advancing twilight that would close the food booths. Joe was delighted when Carey made the decision to close and put out a sign to that effect so that they could begin the uninteresting but unavoidable cleanup process, which, by Carey's admission, was the task she disliked most about her business.

They had worked with dogged diligence for about fifteen minutes at packing up the remaining food and equipment when Carey expressed unexpectedly what had apparently been on her mind during her labors. "We don't know for certain whether Evan saw yesterday's version of the mock battle or the confederate ladies' display."

"Can you think of another reason that he was so irritated yesterday?" Joe asked.

Carey responded airily, "Evan Iverson doesn't need one."

"Doesn't need one what?" came a familiar voice from the other side of the counter at the front of the booth. There stood the subject of the last exchange in the dialogue, looking at Carey and Joe with a furrowed brow.

Joe watched Carey struggling for the right beginning to a response. She began shaking a finger toward Evan as she continued trying to find the words that would be appropriate to her frustration. Joe decided it would be wise to intervene. "We were just wondering what had irritated you so much yesterday that you left before the mock battle even began."

Iverson adopted a look that was the very model of innocence. "Me? Irritated?" he shook his head and looked thoughtful. "I don't recollect any irritation. I watched the mock battle yesterday. You probably got confused because I left the grounds to find a better angle to see it from."

Carey sputtered. "Honestly, Evan, you have absolutely no sense of shame. That pathetic innocence act of yours is sickening."

Iverson tried to look wounded. "I can't imagine what you're talking about."

"Oh, hell no; you wouldn't," Carey fumed. "You're just lucky no one was hurt by your dangerous prank."

Evan turned toward Joe and spread his arms in a gesture of stunned puzzlement. "Do you have any idea what this woman is talking about, Joe?"

"You didn't have anything to do with the unexpected and very dramatic ending to the battle today, Evan?" Joe asked without a trace of accusation.

"No. Was it good?" Evan asked blandly.

Joe had to laugh. "Well, depending on one's point of view, it was either very good or very bad. Personally, I enjoyed it very much."

"I'll bet I would have too. Sorry I missed it," Evan said.

"Idiots," was all Carey muttered and resumed her clean up chores.

"What did you like about it, Joe?" Evan asked. With an air of off hand curiosity.

"It was clearly biased toward the union."

Evan smiled at Joe and pointed his hand in a gun-like gesture. "One nation indivisible."

Joe responded by extending his closed fist toward Even in one of the recent variations of a handshake, "With liberty and justice for all."

"Right on, brother," said Evan and touched his own fist to Joe's

Carey snorted, "You little boys are so cute."

"I didn't come to be made sport of," Evan said with exaggerated loftiness. He then turned serious. "What I did come for is to find Jimmy Chinn. Has he left already?"

"Jimmy hasn't been here all weekend," Carey said. "He told me on Friday he wasn't available to work."

Evan frowned. "He told his grandmother that he was going to work such long hours this weekend that he was going to sleep at the store rather than come home for the night."

"Well, it's not true," Carey stated. "I don't know why he'd say that. It's not like Jimmy to lie."

"Maybe he's doing a little graduation celebrating that he didn't want his grandmother to know about," Joe speculated. "Cutting loose at graduation isn't all that unusual, even for a straight arrow like Jimmy."

"If that's what it is," Evan said with some impatience, "it's very badly timed. There are two recruiters from different universities coming tonight who want to talk to him about accepting a scholarship. I'm talking about major opportunities: Stanford and UCLA, no less. I'm supposed to get him to the high school within a couple of hours from now."

"Then you'd best get busy and look for him," Carey shrugged.

"I wouldn't know where to try next," Evan said. "He's not at home; he hasn't been here and none of his friends have seen him this weekend."

The three of them stood silently for a few moments trying to think of where Evan might look for Jimmy. Their thinking was interrupted by a penetrating voice. "Miss Siebold, I need to speak with you!" They all turned toward the sound and saw Reverend Billy Purefoy bearing down on them purposefully.

Carey looked curious rather than intimidated by the reverend's blustery approach. "This is an unusual honor, reverend. What is it that brings you seek me out for the first time I can remember?"

"I wish it were not necessary to seek you out at all, I assure you, Miss Siebold." He planted himself squarely across the counter from Carey and asked, "Where is my daughter?'

Carey shot Purefoy an unfriendly look. "Reverend, surely you recall informing me just yesterday that you not only have prohibited your daughter from working for me but also of coming anywhere near me. How could I possibly know where she is?"

He stabbed a finger in Carey's direction and growled menacingly, "I will not tolerate your evasiveness, woman. Just tell me where my daughter is."

Both Joe and Evan reacted with a defensive warning sound and took a step in the minister's direction. Carey remained unruffled and gestured to restrain her two protectors. "I resent both your tone and your choice of words, reverend. I have neither seen nor heard from your daughter Honor since you and I last talked.

The combination of Carey's coolness and the protectiveness of her two male friends diminished Reverend Purefoy's aggressiveness, and he said, "Yes, excuse my choice of words, Ms Siebold. Honor's mother and I are very worried. We have not seen her since yesterday morning and no one seems to know her whereabouts. We are most anxious about her welfare. Since you have no information, I will be on my way to pursue other inquiries." With that, Purefoy turned sharply and began to walk away quickly.

Joe smiled. "Sounds like an epidemic of missing high school seniors. Must be a helluva party somewhere."

Carey shook her head in rejection of Joe's notion. "An overnight bash isn't the style of either of those two kids. Jimmy is the most earnest and level-headed young man that I've ever known. And Honor, while she's no saint, as I happen to know, is a very bright girl of good character who is also very careful not to outrage her parents' feelings."

"Well, if it's unlikely that the two of them aren't at some weekend long graduation party," Joe offered, "maybe they're having a more personal celebration, just the two of them. How well do they know each other?"

"I don't think that's it," Evan said. "I don't know when Jimmy would have time to get involved with a girl friend. With working at the store, athletics and his school work, which he takes very seriously, I don't see how he'd have time to get involved in a romance."

"So it's just a coincidence that they're both missing this weekend?" Joe said disbelievingly.

"Having been tied up here all weekend, Joe, we wouldn't have heard about any car accidents," Carey mused.

Evan wondered aloud, "In Jimmy's case, wouldn't his grandmother have heard? I talked to her less than an hour ago, and she's heard nothing from him or about him."

The three stood silently for a moment, unable to speculate further about the whereabouts of the missing young people. Shortly, their attention was drawn toward the highway where several sheriff's cars approached with their roof lights flashing. The three watched as the cars turned into the meadow which had recently been the site of the mock battle. The cars proceeded to the bank of the river and stopped in a row at the near bank. Two uniformed officers emerged from each of the four cars parked at the edge of the bank that had been the refuge of the confederate battle re-enactors.

The officers stood together looking across the river at the bank where the mysterious explosions had taken place that had caused the panic-stricken flight of the rebel performers. The deputies seemed to be searching for a way across the stream to more closely examine the exact spots where the explosions had occurred. Soon they descended the bank in an apparent attempt to make their way over the stream. Since the volume of flow was not heavy at this time of year, the river could normally be crossed on the rocks that protruded above the water surface. That they had succeeded in crossing became apparent as the officers could be seen scrutinizing the bank on the other side of the river.

Evan Iverson broke the silence and said, "You know, the possibility of Jimmy's being in a car accident merits some looking into. I think that I'll go back to his home and ask his grandmother if she's heard anything since I talked to her."

As Even strode quickly away, Joe had to smile, despite his concern for the young people that he was feeling after the discussions of the last ten minutes. He tilted his head toward the rapidly departing Evan Iverson and said to Carey, "With eight sheriff's deputies and their car radios a few hundred feet way, why is Evan going back to town to ask Grandma Chinn if she's heard anything about an accident? The sheriffs would either know or could check in a couple minutes, couldn't they? Could it be that Evan doesn't care to make himself visible to the police looking into the mysterious finish of the mock battle?"

Carey's face broadened with her own smile. "Now you're beginning to understand the bizarre complexities of one Evan Iverson. Carey waved her hand dismissively in the direction Iverson had gone. "Let's finish up here and call it a day. I'm exhausted."

23

WITH THE CLOSING-UP CHORES completed, Joe insisted he follow Carey back to the store to assist in putting away the remaining perishables and, more importantly, to be nearby until she put the considerable amount of money from the day's sales into the store safe. These tasks behind them, Carey invited Joe for a drink to celebrate the end of the strenuous but profitable weekend. Joe was more than ready to relax a bit. Despite their mutual perception when they arrived at Carey's apartment that they were really too tired to eat, they augmented their drinks with a considerable amount of cheese and crusty bread.

They were midway through a second drink when the door bell rang. Joe went down the stairs and opened the door to a broadly smiling Jimmy Chinn and a young woman Joe recognized as having seen once before. Jimmy now introduced her as Honor Purefoy, and asked if they might speak with Carey. Joe let them lead the way upstairs.

At the sight of them Carey uttered a sigh of relief and gestured for them to sit. "People have been asking about both of you. Where have you been?"

Honor's smile was uncharacteristically shy. Jimmy answered with his usual deference but evident decisiveness. "We'll explain in a bit, but we were hoping to ask you something first."

"No," Carey insisted. "First you tell me. Have you been in touch with your parents. Do you have any idea how worried they are?"

"I called my grandmother a little while ago," Jimmy reported.

Carey looked at Honor, who shook her head and said, "Not yet."

"Well, that will have to be the first order of business, Honor," Carey said firmly and pointed toward the kitchen wall. "The phone is right over there." Honor's reluctance to go to the phone was palpable. "Nothing else can happen here until you call, Honor," Carey emphasized.

Honor looked relieved when it was her mother rather than her father who answered the phone. She tersely told her mother where she was and said that she would be home later. She looked quite subdued when she returned to her seat. Honor's atypical meekness caused Carey to study Jimmy intently. Jimmy smiled at Honor for a moment and then turned to face Carey. "Well," he began and then paused for a deep breath, "what I was wondering is whether you would consider hiring me full time in the store after I graduated next week."

Carey's frown showed her surprise at the question. "I was planning on your continuing your part time hours for the summer, Jimmy, just as you have for a couple years. I just assumed you'd be playing baseball again this summer." Carey looked at the young man sympathetically. "Are you worried about the cost of college, Jimmy? Evan tells me you are likely to get an athletic scholarship which will take care of all your expenses."

Jimmy shook his head and lowered his eyes a bit. "I won't be going away on any scholarship, Carey. I'll be staying right here in Craterville or maybe down the road in Santa Clara if I can't find an apartment here."

Carey frowned at this news. "Jimmy, surely it can't be that you're not going to go to college."

"I'm going to go to Santa Clara Junior College to start with. So is Honor," he added with a smiling glance at the pretty blonde sitting beside him.

"Jimmy," Carey spoke the name with a great deal of earnestness, "I've read that Honor is the class valedictorian, and I know that you are somewhere in the top five or ten percent of the graduates. Why would either one of you be going to a junior college rather than some top quality university or college?"

"Because Santa Clara J. C. is what we can afford," Jimmy said.

Joe wondered if Carey was as struck by Jimmy's use of the plural pronoun as he. He knew she had been when she asked, "Jimmy, you two haven't done something very reckless, have you?"

The young pair sat silently and exchanged a look that radiated confidence that was almost defiant. "I wouldn't call it reckless," Honor said, breaking her silence for the first time. "Although no doubt some people would look at it that way."

"We're married," Jimmy contributed. "We gave it lots of thought before we did. We're not making a mistake."

Joe, glad not to be part of the surprising conversation, watched Carey struggle to decide on a response to the unexpected news.

The silence continued until the sound of the door bell was followed by the opening of the door at the bottom of the stairs, which had apparently been left unlocked The tread of hurried footsteps on the stairs was immediate.

Evan Iverson burst into the apartment looking the epitome of frustration. "Jimmy, your grandmother told me you were here. Where have you been, boy? Your coach has been nursemaiding two impatient college recruiters from competing schools who want to convince you to accept a full scholarship. I'm not sure how much longer they will wait to talk to you. We've got to get to the high school in Santa Clara right away."

Jimmy rose from his seat and faced Evan squarely with an expression that hoped for understanding. "Mr. Iverson, I appreciate how much you've done, both improving my performance in the decathlon and using your contacts to get me such an opportunity, but my situation has changed. I wouldn't be able to accept a scholarship offer now."

"Jimmy, we're talking about Stanford and Cal here, two of the finest schools in the world, both offering you a free education," Evan spoke with a stress that assumed that Jimmy had not grasped the implications of what he had been told.

Jimmy nodded affirmatively. "I understand what I'll be passing up, but I've decided to pursue my education and track participation in a different way. I'm going to do two years at Santa Clara J. C. to start. They have a track program. After that I'll see about transferring to a four year school."

"You can't be serious," Evan gasped in disbelief. "Haven't I told you that you've got to look past college. If you participate in a big time collegiate program and compete against the best decathletes in the nation, you have the potential to develop into an Olympic caliber athlete at the time of the first or second Olympic games after you finish college. You won't get that kind of development or opportunity through a junior college program, not to mention the difference in the quality of the education you'll receive."

"Track, academics, whatever," Jimmy answered patiently, "It always comes down to doing the best I can every day. You taught me that." Jimmy spoke with conviction. "Honor and I haven't changed our goals just because we got married. We're just going to work at them differently." As Joe listened to the eighteen year old, he thought Jimmy sounded very sure of himself and his plans. Joe doubted that he had been as mature as the young man seemed when he Jimmy's present age. He recalled his pronouncements then about his life's plans as mostly bravado. He wondered if that was the reality with Jimmy as well.

Evan looked at a loss for words. He glanced back and forth at the two young people as though he was trying to understand an alien life form and then turned to Carey. "Did you have something to do with this?" he accused.

"Of course not," Carey responded dismissively. "I didn't even know they were involved with each other, let alone married, until a few minutes ago."

Evan looked unconvinced. "So there's been no counseling about how a commitment to a goal like the Olympics might end up separating them forever? That they'd be sacrificing their life together?"

Carey sighed contemptuously. "You're being ridiculous. I don't relate every situation to what happened to us. I got over our breakup a long time ago. It's time you did too."

Evan pointed at Carey accusingly. "I didn't give you up. You gave me up."

"Not exactly. By the time you got around to me, I'd lost interest." It was apparent to Joe that Carey spoke without bitterness. She seemed to be stating a long-established fact.

"I guess it couldn't have meant much to you; you got over it so easily," Evan charged.

"Do we really have to do this in front of these people?" Carey asked, eyeing Evan with her annoyance clearly evident.

"Maybe it's time we did," Evan asserted. "Maybe we should have done it years ago."

"It'll be just as pointless now as it would have been then, but if you insist, I'll say what I would have said then. You didn't have to choose between me and four years of training and competing to make the Olympic team. I was willing to take second place to your goal if you just wouldn't shut me out. However, you were so convinced I'd be a distraction that you shelved me totally. 'One and only one big thing at a time,' you said."

"As soon as the Olympics were over, I came for you with the same intensity I'd given to the games," Evan said forcefully.

"I'm not going to bore and embarrass these people with any more of this discussion," Carey said. "All you need to know is that these two young people had no idea that you and I had any history. I've never spoken to them about their plans; I didn't know they had any plans."

Iverson turned his attention to the young couple. "Look. You two should think this over. Lots of scholarship athletes are married nowadays. Believe me, things can be worked out if the school wants you bad enough. Just give it a chance. Talk to these two recruiters." His earnestness was obvious.

Jimmy sat down beside Honor again. He took her hands in his and stared into her eyes questioningly. Honor spoke quietly. "We've talked about this, Jimmy."

Before Jimmy could respond, a loud rapping was heard on the door downstairs.

Joe said he would go. Shortly Reverend Purefoy appeared at the top of the stairs in an obviously agitated state. Joe trailed behind him, struggling to hide his amusement. Purefoy's face was red with anger as he bore down on Carey, "You said you didn't know where my daughter was," he accused. Carey was undaunted by Purefoy's bluster and merely smiled. Joe felt obliged to step in and say, "And when we told you that, it was true."

Carey's bland expression conveyed that she didn't think she needed defending; however, Honor stood and said, "Miss Siebold insisted I call home as soon as we arrived, father."

Purefoy stabbed a finger in his daughter's direction and directed, "I'll not speak to you until we get home, young lady."

As Purefoy turned to address Carey again, Honor said, "Jimmy and I haven't exactly decided where home is going to be, father." She returned to her seat beside her new husband.

Purefoy looked more confused than stunned by his daughter's statement. He looked at the young couple, his brow furrowing as his inferences built around his daughter's words. "What foolishness have you been playing at, girl?"

Jimmy Chinn looked at his father-in-law with the directness and confidence that are possessed by only the young and bold or the mature and unusually successful. "Your daughter and I are married, sir."

It took the minister a long moment to digest what his new son-in-law had said. Joe found that he felt no guilt at enjoying the Reverend Purefoy's obvious discomfiture. No doubt what had happened was drastically different from the father's plans for his daughter's life; however, Joe retained enough romanticism in his heart to think there was a better than average chance that the bright and bold youngsters would make a good life together. If intelligence and commitment were sufficient to make a start, they were starting with better odds that many older, more conventional couples.

"This can't be so," sputtered the Reverend Purefoy.

"We took our vows before the Methodist minister in Santa Clara, father. I think you know him," Honor said calmly, as though a placid presentation with some familiar element would help her father absorb the stunning news.

"Why?" was all the astonished father could respond.

"We're in love. We want to start our life together," said the minister's daughter, her prosaic statement redeemed by her sincerity.

"Yes, yes," her father the minister responded dismissively. "So says everyone who's ever come to me to get married. What I mean is, when we talked recently on intimate matters, you told me you weren't pregnant."

"At the time, I was planning not to be," Honor offered ambiguously. With a smile at her husband, she added simply, "But I am."

It was now Carey and Joe who were surprised. With Joe's assistance, Carey had provided Honor with the medication for terminating the possible pregnancy during the time when it could have been stopped. Joe, and he was sure Carey as well, had assumed that Honor would not have asked for the medication if she did not intend to use it. Of course, there was the possibility that it had been ineffective.

Seeing Carey's confused expression, Honor explained, "I carried the pills with me all day on the day I got them. I wasn't sure what I wanted to do. I knew I wanted to have Jimmy's baby some day. That evening, father, you told me about having heard the rumor that abortion pills were available in Craterville. Remember, you made me swear on the Bible that I'd never take something like that. I can't say that your making me swear was the whole reason I didn't take the pills. What I wanted to choose for me and Jimmy was the main reason. So I didn't take them. I still remember the box. They were packaged like hard candy of a variety of flavors. The wording on the outside said that what was inside was mine to choose. And for single girls who don't want to have a baby and change their lives, I guess they are, unlike the actual hard candy that are called life savers, truly life savers. But for me, they were a life changer because I didn't take them."

Reverend Purefoy glared at his daughter. "And how do you think that you can make a life together, you two, soon to be three, at your age and limited education?"

Jimmy was quick to respond. "We'll work; we'll study; we'll make out."

Evan quickly injected, "It'll be nothing like the future you and Honor are turning your backs on, Jimmy." Joe could see that Evan could not resist renewing his argument, perhaps hoping that the presence of the new father-in-law would renew consideration of the course Evan wanted the young couple to explore.

"I doubt the two of you even know where to begin," Purefoy said contemptuously.

"Actually," Carey began, "that's why they're here. I've been thinking about Jimmy's request for a full time job this summer." Carey turned to the young pair and said, "I'll tell you what I've worked out, Two full time salaries would be a bit too steep for me to handle. But, if you'd accept living here with me as part of your pay, I think that I could use the two of you full time, or close to it, for the summer. We can think about the fall arrangements later when your classes at the junior college are about to start."

"I knew it," Evan muttered, "you had this in mind all along."

"Oh, don't be ridiculous, Evan," Carey dismissed. "I'm just trying to help with the realities of the unexpected situation. Actually, you should do the same. You'd be more helpful if you'd put your efforts into to convincing Jimmy that he should let you help him continue training for the track program at the junior college."

Everson threw up his hands in a sign of surrender. "I need to think," he said and disappeared down the stairs without another word.

The pleased expressions on the faces of the newlyweds made it possible for the three remaining adults to anticipate what the pair's answer would be to Carey's proposal.

"Well, Honor," Reverend Purefoy began petulantly, "since it appears that you have decided not to make your home with your mother and me, you may as well begin your new life immediately. You will no longer be welcome in my home. Your mother will pack your belongings. You may pick them up tomorrow, if you wish."

Honor looked stricken by her father's dictate. "I don't want to lose you and mother because of my marriage, father," she pleaded.

"That is a choice that you have made," Purefoy said coldly. "You can be a member of you husband's family now." He said the last as though he considered it a punishment.

"Unfortunately, sir, my grandmother is no happier than you are about our marriage," reported Jimmy. "We hoped you'd be more understanding."

"Give your grandmother my compliments on her good sense," muttered Purefoy as he started for the stairs with a curt nod to Carey.

For a short time, Carey and Joe joined Jimmy in consoling Honor over her distress at her father's cutting her off from contact with her mother. They had some success in assuring her that her mother was unlikely to agree with her father's insistence on ending the family relationship. Honor knew her father's domineering nature and was dubious.

A dampened atmosphere fell over the group briefly, but then Carey set the newlyweds busy at re-arranging her work room to become their bedroom. She had her desk and files moved into the living room and had other things moved to the storage space behind the grocery store. All that remained was the bed, dresser and single chair that furnished Carey's guest room until clutter began to expand. Before long, it seemed to Joe that the young pair were happier than they had a right to be in view of their circumstances. That, he decided, was the power of love.

Joe was sitting on a chair opposite Carey, who had stretched out on the couch while her guests made themselves a nest for the immediate future. "I was wondering," he began with more than a little hesitancy. "How you feel about your apartment becoming the honeymoon suite."

"Under the circumstances, I think we may say that their honeymoon has past, Joe," Carey said with a tired smile.

"Still," Joe began, his amusement evident in his tone, "they are young and energetic and now free to express their ardor fully."

Carey sat up, showing her awakening to a new implication of sharing space with the newly married nineteen year olds. "Oh, my," Carey said with a mixture of amusement and concern, "too much exposure to youthful passion would be a bit awkward."

"I do have a suggestion," said Joe.

"Which is?"

"You could stay at the cabin with me."

Carey looked thoughtful. She smiled in a moment and said, "I can see some interesting possibilities, My new apartment mates would be close at hand to open the store bright and early and handle things when I wanted some time off. I could have a pleasant summer. Lots of free time to do whatever."

"So you'll do it? Come stay, that is?" Joe asked, taking a major effort to appear unexcited.

"Of course, you have only the one bedroom," Carey mused.

"And the couch in the living area that opens into a bed," Joe added. Then, when he noted Carey's skepticism, he added, "Which is where I would sleep."

"That's terribly accommodating of you," Carey smiled.

"I just thought you'd prefer not to spend your time pretending not to notice the unbridled passion of youth," Joe explained.

Carey came around the low table between the couch and Joe's chair. She sat on the arm of the chair and smiled down at him. "You got something against passion, Joe?"

"No," Joe answered with exaggerated seriousness, "I'm one of its biggest advocates between the right people at the right time."

"I've known you for a while now, Joe," Carey said with a bit of prodding in her tone, "and I've begun to wonder if you had any interest in that particular emotion."

"You just haven't seen me at the right time," Joe said with a broad grin.

"When would that be, Joe?"

"Oh," Joe said with an air of speculating thoughtfully despite any need for such weighty consideration, "suppose we start to share the cabin and I propose modifying the sleeping arrangement. That might lead to my exhibiting such passion as would surprise you."

"Why Joseph Bell," Carey said feigning horror, "Such an idea-- and from a man who hasn't so much as kissed me."

"If you weren't so damn hard to understand where that and related activity is concerned, I'd have done it long ago."

"Oh, you lie, Joe Bell. You've been so focused on your work that I've made no impact on you at all."

"Or maybe I've had too many experiences at avoiding emotional bruising to make my feelings obvious."

Carey stood and said, "I can see that this is going to take a lot more consideration. Why don't I throw some things in a bag, and we'll tell the lovebirds we're leaving."

Joe stood. "Don't be long," he said.

Carey laughed. "The man is so eager to talk."

Joe smiled broadly. "No, the time for talking is almost passed."